SECRETS *of* GREYMOOR

SECRETS *of* GREYMOOR

CLARA GILLOW CLARK

CANDLEWICK PRESS

Copyright © 2009 by Clara Gillow Clark

First edition 2009

Library of Congress Cataloging-in-Publication Data

Clark, Clara Gillow.
Secrets of Greymoor / Clara Gillow Clark. — 1st ed.
p. cm.
Sequel to: Hattie on her way.
Summary: As her grandmother's financial situation worsens, Hattie is forced to attend a "common school," in late nineteenth-century Kingston, New York, where she stands up to a show-off, shares embellished stories about life as a rich girl, and tries to recover her family's wealth.
ISBN 978-0-7636-3249-6
[1. Wealth—Fiction. 2. Grandmothers—Fiction. 3. Schools—Fiction.
4. Kingston (N.Y.)—History—19th century—Fiction.] I. Title.
PZ7.C5415Se 2009
[Fic]—dc22   2008019063

2 4 6 8 10 9 7 5 3 1

Printed in the United States of America

This book was typeset in Stempel Schneidler.

Candlewick Press
99 Dover Street
Somerville, Massachusetts 02144

visit us at www.candlewick.com

In loving memory of my parents
Lee and Naomi Gillow

To live in hearts we leave behind is not to die.

Chapter One

I could hear a constant jingling of harness bells in the avenue and the voices of girls calling gaily to each other as they arrived in their sleighs and carriages at the big blue house next door. The neighbor girl, Ivy Victoria Blackmore Vandermeer, was having a costume party, but I wasn't going. I couldn't go. I hadn't been invited.

There was a good reason for that: I had threatened to scalp Ivy Victoria with an ax after she'd told me that my grandfather had been murdered. Murdered, she said, and planted in the vegetable garden by Grandmother and Buzzard Rose, the cook. That's what her mother had told her, she said, and I believed it to be a true fact, because Grandfather had been a big mystery back when I first came here to live.

Nobody had ever wanted to talk about Grandfather. Not before, when my mother was alive in our little cabin over the mountains. Not here, after my pa brought me to live temporarily with Grandmother in her fancy gingerbread house. I believed Grandfather had been murdered until Grandmother took me to see him in the Utica Insane Asylum, where he'd been since before I was born and since he'd lost most of Grandmother's fortune and heard voices talking to him in the walls.

Then in December, he up and died. The telegram came right after Christmas, and Grandmother, who always wore pale lavender, put on black and a sorrowful face.

Everyone knew the truth about Grandfather now. Ivy's father had even come to pay his respects to Grandmother. But he was the only one who had.

After that, Ivy often watched me from her bedroom window. Did that mean that she wanted to be friends? Maybe. But maybe not enough to invite me to her party. I was pretty sure that her mother would not allow it. Mrs. Vandermeer wasn't the kind, forgiving sort.

I sighed and pretended not to notice all the happy

party hullabaloo. It wasn't easy, though, especially since Mr. Horace Bottle, my tutor, was agog over the event.

Horace now let the drapery fall over the dining-room window for about the eighty-seventh time. "The cakes, the confections, the lovely costumes," he said wistfully. Being left out was much harder for Horace than for the rest of us. He loved tables weighted down with cakes and confections. He loved watching people, and he loved the ladies and the girls in their colorful gowns with tiers of Swiss lace, their pink arms, their graceful necks, their baubles. "It's a costume ball," he said in a loud whisper, "spring flowers peeking out of dark winter capes. Do come and look, Hattie." He pulled back the drapery even more. "Most delightful to see bright blossoms on a winter's day when clouds do nothing but drag their bellies over us like fat, squashing gods."

Reluctantly I went over to watch with Horace. Girls in costumes and flowered bonnets paraded up the walk — a pansy, a daisy, a tiger lily, a daffodil. A bright-faced Ivy Victoria stood at the door, blue flowers sewn to her gown, a garland of ivy sprinkled with blue paper flowers on her head, her yellow hair arranged in soft waves, her fat sausage curls gone. She handed each flower-topped girl a slip of paper as she passed through the door.

3

"Conundrums. I do love the challenge of a good mind puzzler," Horace said with a delighted hush just as Grandmother popped her head around the corner, her face anxious-looking.

"Teatime," she said. "Cinnamon and nutmeg, nuts in the warm sweet buns." Grandmother was a pale, twittery songbird, and when things took a bad turn (or just an unexpected one), she usually worried the lace on her cuffs and collar or the folds of her skirt, or fingered the cameo brooch pinned at her throat, or knitted her fingers together over and over. Today, though, her fingers were quiet. Since the telegram of Grandfather's death, her hands had been still, sad as birds at night, waiting for the sun to come up again.

"Warm sweet buns? Cinnamon? Scrumptious . . . sublime," Horace said. Inhaling deeply, he turned away from the window and the festivities next door. Dropping the drapery, he sprinted off.

I stood there a moment longer, peeking through the panels of heavy fabric. Suddenly Ivy looked over at Grandmother's house, stared as if she knew someone was watching—and why wouldn't she? Horace had pretty near pressed his nose to the windowpane ever

4

since the deliveries had begun this morning. I held my breath, motionless, clenching the dark drapery, hoping she wouldn't see me. Her smile faded. She bent her head, twisted away, and went inside.

"Hattie, dear?" Grandmother had come back and was standing right behind me. She touched my arm.

"It's snowing," I said. Cold white flakes were flying against the windowpane and sticking.

She rested a hand on my shoulder now. "I wish you could go to parties as I did, and your mother. I wish . . . oh, once upon a time, things were so different." Her voice dipped to a forlorn whisper, ending with a sad, fluttery sigh. All her thoughts had taken flight to once-upon-a-time. "Do you mind very much?" she said gently.

"Not very much, Grandmother," I said, letting the drapery panel fall back against the window. "I just wanted to see." But I did mind. Very much. I wanted to be one of those flowers bobbing up the walk—not a pale lily, but a tiger lily. I wanted to play games and conundrums, laugh and share secrets. A savage pang of longing snarled in my chest. I was desperate for a friend, someone my own age, a girl, any girl at all. It was my secret, something I didn't want the others to know. It would make Grandmother sad. She would worry that she had failed me, and I didn't want Grandmother to be sad or worry any more than she had to.

Grandmother smiled faintly. "Let's have our tea then, shall we?"

"I'll be right there, Grandmother," I said. When she left, I pulled the drapery back once more and watched as more laughing flowers bobbed up the walk. And then came the sudden thumping of footsteps on the front porch, and the clink of the brass letter slot as something was shoved through. An invitation? *I wasn't forgotten after all.* Heart thrumming excitedly, I raced to the front hall and snatched up the smooth white envelope. With shaky fingers, I slowly turned it over. *Please, please, please . . .* I wished. But it was not an invitation. It was nothing good at all. Stamped in bold black print in the corner was CITY OF KINGSTON — TAX COLLECTION — PAYMENT OVERDUE.

I sucked in my breath and peered through the glass. The postman was gone. His single, telltale prints marked the fresh snow on the porch, down the steps, and along the walk to the street. But the snow was falling thick and fast now; the wind swept across the porch. In no time, the boot treads would be covered over.

The bell for tea clinked impatiently. I pressed the

letter against my chest. PAYMENT OVERDUE sounded bad. Poor, dear Grandmother had had money worries since long before I came to live here. Her only source of income was from the shipping business she'd inherited from her father, but business hadn't been good this past year. Then she'd been melancholy with the news of Grandfather's death. And now the party next door was a sad reminder that we were forgotten by society. What would Grandmother do if I gave her the letter now? Her face would go pale; she'd tap her chest nervously and fret horribly. Rose's special cinnamony treat would be spoiled, and all of us, even Horace, would sink into a cloudy gloom.

It wouldn't hurt to wait a bit longer to give her the letter. I gave a wild look around and darted over to the gilt-framed mirror that went clear to the floor.

With shaky fingers, I hurriedly stuffed the letter behind it, out of sight. I heard the whoosh as it slid down the wall and caught on something. Stuck. Halfway to nowhere and out of my reach. I tried to peek back there, but to my horror I discovered that the mirror was securely bolted to the wall. Trembling and feeling a little sick, I rushed down the hall to the library before anyone came looking for me.

Chapter Two

Just as we had every other day since I had come here to live, we gathered in the library for afternoon tea and ginger cakes. Warm, sugary cinnamon buns were a special treat, and I guessed that old Rose the cook was trying to make up for my not getting invited to the party. I was just glad Rose was busy pouring tea when I came in breathless. If she had looked at me, she would have guessed right away that I had been up to something.

"Common school tomorrow, Hattie," Grandmother said once I was settled in my usual place next to her on the chaise. Horace and Rose sat in twin wing chairs, the low table of tea things between us, the pleasant *shush* of gaslights and the solid ticking of clocks behind us. Grandmother sounded forlorn, and her hands lay clasped and silent in her lap. She had planned for me to go to Kingston Academy one day, as soon as Horace had caught me up on all the required studies for entrance into secondary school. That hadn't happened yet, and hard times had made it necessary for Horace to find a teaching position in a common school and for me to be enrolled in one. Unfortunately, we were not at the same one.

"Madame Greymoor, it is a good common school. Some excellent faculty," Horace said soothingly as he helped himself to another bun. "She'll be ready for the Academy by semester's end, and, really, she has time. No reason to rush our girl."

Mr. Horace Bottle had been my tutor right up till the holidays, and he was like one of the family now. He was the easiest among us to like, maybe because he himself had so few dislikes. I was a picky eater, but Horace didn't just eat; he savored each bite, tasted it for its own special flavor—even things like cooked cabbage or raisins. He was tall and, despite his relish for eating, still as skinny as a hollyhock.

Grandmother was not soothed. "Only commoners go to common school. We are not commoners." She sighed.

9

"Still, Hattie's education cannot, must not, be neglected. It is only a temporary measure."

"Hmpf," Rose grumbled with her usual scowling gruffness. "Mark my words, Hortensia—she'll be catching some dread disease." Rose may have been the cook, but she was much more like a sister to Grandmother because they had been together almost forever. Rose always wore black and a gloomy air, and she looked like a buzzard. She couldn't see the bright side of anything even when she tried, which wasn't often.

Grandmother sighed again. "Hard to believe that we've come to this. If my father were alive . . ." Grandmother's father, Nathaniel Holmes, was revered and remembered for bringing wealth, social standing, and happiness to the family, but Grandmother's husband, my grandfather, William Greymoor, had lost pretty much all of those things.

As for me, I was desperate to go to common school, because it meant I was going to make friends. It would be different this time, not like when I'd met Ivy Victoria. She'd told me I looked like a boy because my hair was so short. She said I talked funny, too. But my hair was longish now, and I didn't talk as funny or tell scary lies. I was not about to threaten anyone with an ax either, and I

10

would watch out for my fiery tongue and ways. No matter what.

"If you don't like it, dear . . ." Grandmother said suddenly. "If things don't go well . . . If anything does not please you . . ."

"Don't worry, Grandmother," I said warmly. "If anything goes wrong, if anything bad happens, I'll come straight home to you and Rose."

Grandmother brightened, but worry still puckered her pale eyebrows. Grandmother never forgot, not even for the space between ticks on the clock, that I was on loan from Pa and that he'd brought me here, mainly, to get the best schooling. That's why I had come. But I had stayed because Grandmother needed me to love her a whole lot. She had lost too many things and too many people already.

"But you will try, Hattie," Grandmother said anxiously.

"You must," said Horace.

I nodded slowly, my head lowered so the old ones and Horace couldn't see in my face how very much I wanted to go to common school.

Chapter Three

The schoolroom smelled of linseed oil and chalk, wet shoe leather and drying wool. I was given a desk in the middle of the room, a slate, a battered McGuffey reader, and a blue Webster book for spelling. After the morning prayer, the teacher read a very long psalm from the Bible while I looked everyone over real good. Most of the girls wore strong brown dresses that looked as if they were made from the same Butterick pattern and same bolt of cloth. My dress was wool the color of claret. That's what Horace told me. Nothing was a simple color like red or yellow or blue to Horace. He taught me to see the many shades of color even in freshly fallen snow.

Except for one boy, I was taller than anybody in the sixth grade. But I didn't look like a boy anymore, not like when I'd first come to Grandmother's and my hair had been chopped off short. I looked like a girl now. I had a real good feeling that I could make friends here, because I had never seen so many girls my own age all together in one place before, not even half.

Before, in the school back home in Pepacton, I was picked on for being a Hill Hawk, different from the children who lived in town or on farms in the valley. Most Hill Hawks didn't bother about school at all. They kept to themselves, lived in the woods in cabins or shanties. Loners, like hawks nesting in high places, Pa told me. Not like folks in the river valley, who stuck together like pitch to a pine tree, he said.

But when Pa took me to work in the woods and I met Jasper, we were friends right off, real easy, like water flowing along smooth and happy in the river. After, when I came to Grandmother's, Mr. Horace Bottle was my friend right off, too. Not instant but quick enough, no fuss or bother. I hoped it could be like that here, too.

The teacher, Miss Finster, was short and round like a little lumpy mole in a soft gray dress, gray hair parted in the middle and pulled straight back into a tight knot.

She squinted, peering at everything as if she'd lost something.

"Lettie, come up to Miss Finster's desk, please," the teacher said.

For a minute I was confused, then realized that Miss Finster was talking about herself as if she were *two* people. Then I had to press a hand to my mouth to keep from laughing aloud. My shoulders shook with laughter as I looked around the room and wondered which rude girl was not paying attention. But all of them were. Faces forward, hands folded on desks in front of them. No one was laughing. No one moved.

"Lettie!" the teacher said. Her chins and cheeks quivered and her face turned red.

Lettie? Hattie? Did she mean me? Nobody moved, so I stood up. "Begging your pardon, ma'am," I said with a little curtsy, "my name is Hattie Belle."

"Come forward," she said, ignoring my correction. "Stand on this line." While I walked to the front of the room, she began to write on the blackboard. When she was finished, she turned around and clapped her hands together to get rid of the chalk dust. "Translate this sentence of Latin for the class."

"Into what language, please?" I asked, since Horace could never make up his mind. Horace loved words spoken in many tongues, the way he loved shades of color.

I saw her calculating squint. "Greek," she said. "Write it on the board."

I swallowed hard. Greek was one of those languages with funny-looking letters and strange words that weren't even halfway easy to pronounce but were fun to look at.

Miss Finster crossed her arms over her waist, her lips all smug-looking at the corners. Heart thudding, I stepped up to the board and began to write slowly, thinking Latin to English, English to Greek.

My hand shook and beads of sweat popped up on my scalp. I began a slow journey of Greek across that blackboard. I could hear the clock ticking, and Miss Finster's heavy breathing.

"Commendable, Lettie," she said, her smug look changing to a warm smile when I was only halfway done. Even though she looked nearly as beamish as Grandmother at me, I figured it was better not to correct her about my name this time. I took my seat.

"Hah! What's so great about that?" someone behind me muttered. "Betcha Aggie could do that."

Who was Aggie? I gulped. Didn't they all know Greek? I was only doing what Horace had taught me to catch me up and prepare me for the Academy one day.

Miss Finster's squinty scowl returned. "Greek, you should know, Lettie, isn't something we learn on this grade level. But our scholars will know Greek. Someday. Perhaps." Miss Finster sounded doubtful; her voice trailed off.

But the word *perhaps* stayed in the air, hung over the room like a sword, and dropped. I could hear the sickle sound as a red-faced, copper-haired girl whirled around and gave me a dark look.

"Can *you* do long division?" a voice hissed quietly from close by.

I could. And square roots, and some algebra. But I bit my lip to keep from hissing something sassy right back.

"Hush your mouths," Miss Finster scolded. "It's time for recitation. Agnes Sykes, please come up and recite 'Charge of the Light Brigade' for us."

The copper-haired girl skipped to the front. She swished her hair and tilted her head up in a proud-like way. Aggie was good. Aggie was dramatic. Even Horace would have been impressed by her expression with hands and voice. Aggie was the class star and a show-off.

When she was done, she minced back to her seat, smiling around at the class. Then her eyes rested on me, and her smile turned smug, a tiny curl to her lip, as if she had showed me up good. I swallowed. I didn't need to prove I was best; I wanted to make friends.

Chapter Four

At recess the girls circled me like a ring-around-the-rosy by the brick wall of the school.

"So, smart girl," Aggie said. She had large eyes as green as mine were blue, hair as curly as mine was straight. Except for her big coppery hair, she was tiny all over, like a pixie in one of the books in Grandmother's library at home, one of the little creatures who picked on giants like me. It was clear enough by the way the girls swarmed around her like honeybees how anxious they were to please her.

I held my sharp, sassy tongue and waited.

"Do you want to join my gang?" she asked. It sounded like a challenge.

Gang? Were all the girls in her gang? "Maybe. What do I have to do?" I said, disinterestedly studying my nails, hoping the girls couldn't see the pounding in my chest. It wouldn't do to let Aggie know how desperate I was for friends. I had been overeager to meet Ivy, trotted right up to her like a happy, tail-wagging pup, but things had not gone too well. And Ivy wasn't even a big show-off.

"Something," she said. "Not much."

Not much sounded suspicious to me. "So, what is it?"

On all sides the other girls watched me.

"Yes or no?" she asked.

"Maybe," I repeated. "Maybe not."

"Maybe your dress is nicer than mine. Nicer than everybody's. Give it to me."

My dress had been a handmade gift from Grandmother and Horace and Rose for Christmas. It was a soft wool trimmed with satin ribbons and lace. If Aggie wanted it, she'd have to rip it off my back. "I won't," I said calmly, trying not to panic.

"Snob Hill girl showing off her Greek and her best dress," Aggie sang.

"Showing off," came the chorus around her.

Snob Hill was news to me, but with a sinking feeling I understood that they thought I had something they

19

didn't and that made me an enemy, unless I obeyed Aggie. And that was not about to happen. So what if they didn't know about the hard times at Grandmother's or that I was really a Hill Hawk from a little cabin with a dirt floor in a hemlock woods? They didn't know I was fierce, either. So far, they didn't know anything about me at all. "I live with my grandmother," I said politely.

"And you think you're better than us in your red dress." Aggie took a step closer. Her hard eyes shone like a cat's in the dark. "My pa is a constable," she said. It sounded like a threat.

I had wanted to be nice, but I didn't want to be bullied. I leaned toward her. "I'm not afraid of you," I said coolly. "Or your father."

Aggie's head snapped up in surprise. They all looked surprised. I saw belief in their faces—and awe. I warmed to it. Warmed to the power. A smoldering ember inside me burst into sudden flame. "Besides, my dress isn't red," I explained. "It's claret. And I will not give it to you. It would be silly of me to do that. Silly and dumb." I stopped to give her a withering Grandmother look before going on. "It wouldn't fit you, and it clashes with your hair. Poor fashion sense, my dear," I said, tutting like Horace.

I stopped and waited, awed by my own self and the strange words that had tumbled out of my mouth. They weren't my sort of words at all. I sounded like Horace with Grandmother's touch of frost. I sounded like a snob. It worked. I saw the other girls eyeing Aggie. I saw clear enough that Aggie might not seem so smart and important to them now.

The girl next to Aggie timidly took a step closer to me. She had soft, kind eyes like a sheep's. She was pretty soft-looking all over, sort of like a potato dumpling. "Do you really live up there?" she said in a hushed tone. She pointed to the hill section, where the mansions lined the avenue like proud kings overlooking the vassals below.

Aggie frowned. A thoughtful, calculating look flickered in her eyes. She stepped closer to the girl who had come forward and linked an arm through hers. "Of course she does, Effie." Aggie's tongue darted out and licked the corners of her mouth. "Don't mind what I said." She was smart all right, smart enough to know that the flock could peck out her eyes as easily as twitter if someone was strong enough to take her place. Aggie shrugged. "New girls all get treated the same. You don't really have to do anything to be in the gang. We all want to be your friend."

I nodded slowly and looked over at the brown sparrows flocked together, little beaks open, eager, waiting for me to throw them crumbs. "Yes, Effie," I said, feeling a bit guilty at deceiving her, "I do live up there." It was the truth, but it felt like a lie. I wasn't born up there, and except to Grandmother, I didn't belong.

They stood breathless with wonder, eyes glazed, arms limp as broken wings. Except for Aggie. For a second her eyes snapped fire, and then she stared hard at the ground as if she were willing it to open up and swallow me. But the other girls, they wanted to touch the world up there, out of reach like a fairy tale with a princess in a castle. They wanted me to be the princess. They wanted the fairy tale. And I would give it to them.

Chapter Five

My fairy tale began with lunch. Everyone watched as I carried my box lunch to my desk. It was the perfect lunch box for a society girl—small and fragile-looking, painted with delicate garden roses in shades of pink that would flatter my dresses and look striking carried next to my indigo cloak. Horace had made it for me, and Grandmother and Rose had approved. On the desks around me were brown sacks or old tin pails that used to have peanut butter in them. I had wanted a paper sack, but now I saw the value of my rose box. It fit the fairy tale.

Unhurriedly, I took my seat. I unhooked the brass latch of the box. I took out a linen napkin and laid it across my lap. I took out a second napkin and spread it on my desk for a tablecloth. I took out a silver fork and china saucer that had lost its cup. Rose had packed little sandwich wedges—neat triangles with the crusts cut off—filled with a meaty pâté. My orange was already peeled and separated into segments. I had thin slices of cheese and a ginger-almond cake.

The others ate without taking their eyes off me. I pressed my lips together to keep from giggling. No one, not ever, had watched me because I was doing something extraordinary. I had always been stared at suspiciously, as if I was bound to say or do something wrong or a little scary.

But not here. Here I was the princess. I took small bites the way Ivy Victoria would, making sure to chew with my mouth closed, elbows off the desk, one arm firmly anchored to my lap. Daintily, I patted my lips with the napkin, gently wiped the corners of my mouth. No jiggling or swinging of feet, no slumping, no slurping or burping, even though no one was around to sharply correct my manners. I could do it. It was fun. It was like having a westerly wind, warmed by the sun, blow straight across me. I shivered from its warmth.

Out of the corner of my eye, I caught Effie copying me. She wasn't making fun of me; she was serious. No one had ever copied me before. When I nibbled on one of my triangle sandwiches, I stuck out my pinky even though I was not using it to balance a bone china teacup. Effie did the same. It was hard to squelch the bubbles of laughter. But I did. Effie was okay. A part of me was sorry for fooling her this way.

"Would you like some of my sandwich?" I asked.

"What's in it?" she asked.

"Pâté de foie gras," I said. I saw ears prick up all around me and Aggie's head twist around.

"Oh." Effie's mouth went round in awe. "Yes . . . please," she said.

I handed over a wedge, and then another. I was a poor, picky eater, and I wasn't particularly fond of goose liver. But Effie was.

I caught a whiff of Effie's flapjack, drizzled with molasses, the leftovers of her breakfast, which she was now happy to forget. My mouth watered. It smelled like home. Like Pa. For a second I felt sick all over, knowing how awful disappointed Pa would be in my show-off shenanigans. It wasn't easy to shut out thoughts as big and clear as Pa's. But I did. Effie wanted to be my friend. She wanted to be like me, and that was scarcer than goose feathers on a brown trout.

"But what is it, what you said?" Aggie had come down the aisle and squeezed in next to Effie. Aggie didn't take up much room, but she filled space real good with her bossy mouth and ways.

I swallowed. "It's French," I said. "A delicacy."

Effie grinned and quickly stuffed the second piece into her mouth, probably so she didn't have to share with Aggie.

Aggie leaned across the aisle and stared at my lunch. "Gaw," she said. "You've got a china plate and a real silver fork."

"It's only a saucer whose cupmate got broken. It's chipped, see?" I said, turning the plate to show her. But the chip was smaller than a fingernail moon and the fork was polished to a soft glow.

I was thinking about offering her a few orange slices when she said, "So, why are you here? In school, I mean, with all of us?" She said it nice enough, but her eyes were fixed a little too hard on my face for me to feel real good about it.

I should have told the truth right then and there. But I took one look at Effie's glowing face, and I didn't. I couldn't. She loved the fairy tale, relished it the way Horace relished food, savoring each little bite.

I opened my mouth and out came something I didn't plan to say at all. "My grandmother is in mourning." I lowered my head and looked sorrowful, relieved that what had popped out of me wasn't a lie, not a whole lie anyway. It was true enough so that I didn't have to feel real uncomfortable about it in my conscience, but it wasn't any sort of real answer.

"Sorry," Effie said with a gasp.

Aggie didn't say "sorry." Aggie was quiet. Death was a huge, dark power that nobody much wanted to mess with. Death was nothing to scoff at. I sighed, relieved and temporarily grateful to Death for rescuing me.

And that was the end of questions. But not the end of the fairy tale, I'm ashamed to say. I picked up my silver fork and began to eat my ginger-almond cake with the regal manner befitting a true princess and watched as the wonder of it cast a spell over the others.

Chapter Six

That afternoon when I walked home from school, the grand houses along the avenue seemed friendly, with their wraparound porches, high-hatted turrets and towers, their painted dresses the colors of spring—pinks, lilacs, periwinkles . . . Today when I walked past, each house seemed charmed to see me. Today I was a princess, and I belonged here in one of these smiling castles.

I was at Grandmother's gate ready to lift the latch when I caught the flutter of a curtain in the house next door. I whirled around so my red dress flashed out of my dark cloak like a cardinal's wings in an evergreen tree, swung so if Ivy was looking, she would get a real good look at my dress and my fancy rose-painted box. I glanced up. Yup, Ivy Victoria was there all right, staring down at me, squashed like a yellow bug against the windowpane of her big blue house. I stared back just as bold, even though I no longer had the joyful feeling that I'd carried with me from school. She could look down on me all she wanted. Why should I care? I had friends at school now.

But I waved anyhow, turned quickly, and headed up the walk, afraid to see if she didn't wave back. Ivy Victoria wouldn't know whether to wave without asking permission from her mother, but that was no excuse for me to be unfriendly or rude.

When I stepped inside, something went *squoosh* underfoot. It was a letter from the afternoon mail, and now I'd left a soggy footprint on it. At the sight of the white envelope, my heart flipped over like a flapjack and sank right down to somewhere around my knees. I eased the door shut, hoping Grandmother and Rose hadn't heard me come in. Bending down to pick the letter off the hall rug, I began to wish: *Please, please, not another tax notice. Please, not a bill for anything.*

To my relief, the letter was addressed to Mr. Horace

Bottle from Kingston Academy. It had to be good news, or at least not bad news like a big bill for coal or city gas. I was curious all right, but the envelope was extra superior and heavyweight paper with no chance of seeing through it to what was inside. I set Horace's mail on the hall table for him and headed for the kitchen.

I didn't mean to eavesdrop, but when I heard the serious voices coming from the library, I slowed way down and stopped out of sight but close enough to hear. I got a funny feeling about doing that, but somber talk meant something secret and important that they wouldn't talk about in front of me, and I wanted to know what was going on.

"Whatever shall I do with William's things?" I heard Grandmother say. "I always believed that he'd come home well again, and he'd need his good tailored suits, these kid gloves, monogrammed shirts, handkerchiefs, but now. . . ." Her voice trailed off.

"Give them to charity," Rose said. "There's nobody here could get use of them."

"If only Horace weren't so tall. I don't know . . ." Grandmother faltered. "They're quite out of style, probably worth next to nothing now. Such good fabric, though . . . They might bring something, but, oh, how awful to think of dear William's things sold at any price. Even worse to think of them given away to be worn by someone unsuitable, of low station, who wouldn't appreciate the value. . . . Tatters in no time."

"Maybe," Rose said. "But a poor man wouldn't mind the cold so much in a woolen suit. He'd value that, I'd say."

"A poor man is no less rich than we these days, Rose," Grandmother said with a heavy sigh.

Grandmother's words made my heart sink. If she said we were no better off than a poor man, we were even worse off than I'd thought. I backed softly away from the door, but I still heard Rose say, "Hmpf, Hortensia, what could you possibly know of a pauper's lot?"

And then silence. I sucked in my breath and let it out slowly. Grandmother had hard times, but she was no pauper, not even close. Rose was right about that. I made noise in the hall and clattered into the library to make it seem as if I'd just gotten home.

The two looked caught.

"My goodness," Grandmother said. "I didn't realize the time." She flushed a telltale pink and patted her lap nervously. Clearly, she hadn't intended for me to discover them going through Grandfather's belongings.

"I'll just put the kettle on," Rose said, getting up.

I couldn't look Grandmother in the eye. Instead, I grabbed up a soft coat and slipped it on. It was only a little big. I was tall for my age, but Grandfather was a lot smaller than I'd thought. "What are you going to do with these?" I asked innocently.

Grandmother looked a bit flustered. "Why, I . . ."

"We could alter them, couldn't we, like we did with Ma's gown for me? But into a lady's suit, for you?" I picked up a pair of black trousers. "Hmm . . . rip out the inside leg seams . . . fashion it into a skirt. Maybe not . . ." I said, trailing off, not quite able to see how that could work. But Horace would know.

"Ingenious, Hattie, dear," Grandmother said. "You've hit on the perfect solution. I do need a proper walking suit." Black for mourning, she meant. "Even though I don't go out much these days." She smiled. "I am most gratified, dear," she said, laying aside some of Grandfather's shirts. "I'm off to tell Rose and help her with the tea things."

Then I was alone. I brushed my hands over the rich cashmere of the suit and felt a slight bump beneath my left hand. Frowning, I checked inside. There was a slit in the lining, a hidden pocket. I pushed a hand down inside and pulled out a thin leather book, so small it seemed made just for secrets and hiding. My fingers trembled as I pressed back the cover and looked inside.

Chapter Seven

I stared at the small, neat printing in Grandfather's book. I leafed through page after page. It was all carefully set down, hand-printed nonsense. No real words or even letters. Gibberish. I flopped down on the chaise and dropped the book in my lap. I watched the afternoon sun sink out of sight.

Huffing a little in disappointment, I picked up the book again. There was printing on the cover along the bottom edge. Squinting, I tried to make out the letters, but they were faded. I ran my fingers over the spot and felt depressions of letters where the nib of the pen had dug into the soft black leather. I took the book over to the window, tilted it in the light, and the words became clear. On the cover, Grandfather had printed, MY TREASURE.

My heart fluttered excitedly. He'd written the word *treasure* in all capital letters. I opened the book again and studied the printing closely now. It wasn't gibberish. The page was filled with rows of letters written backward. Maybe they were clues to a hidden treasure. Why else bother to be so mysterious? Everyone thought that Grandfather had lost Grandmother's fortune through bad business deals, but instead of losing it, maybe he'd squirreled it away. My heart beat wildly now as I imagined finding a lost fortune right here in this house.

I heard the front door bang closed and the rattle of the tea cart coming down the hall. I slipped the book back inside the pocket. For now, I would keep it a secret. I would figure out the code, find the fortune, and present it all to Grandmother along with the news about the tax notice behind the mirror. Then there would be money for taxes. For servants. For furniture and paintings to fill up the empty rooms again. For good things I could not even imagine. It was a good plan. Ingenious.

"Good news. Good news," Horace sang as he danced into the room behind Grandmother and Rose. He was pink-cheeked and giddy and holding his letter.

Once we were all in our usual places, Horace gave each of us a notable nod, but he waited until tea was poured to share his news. "As you know," he said, sure of our attention now, "I applied to many schools before the holidays, and I had the good fortune of being interviewed at the academies. Alas, the position I secured was at a common school, but things have changed. Yes, indeed," he crowed, waving the letter in front of him. For once his tea cake was untouched after the rest of us had already taken bites of our own. "There was a sudden, well, vacancy," Horace said (which probably meant someone had died), "and as of Monday next, I begin teaching languages at Kingston Academy. Quite a rise in salary and a feather in my cap, if I must say so myself."

"Well done, Horace," I said, pleased. Treasure seemed to be falling into our laps today.

"Lucky to get you, I'd say," Rose said.

"You may know that Governor DeWitt Clinton attended Kingston Academy," Grandmother said, looking very pleased with the news.

"I will have many scholars destined for greatness." Horace smoothed the pages of his letter. "It says I am to meet with the dean on Friday to go over my duties. Afterward, I will be introduced to the faculty and my classes," he said breathlessly. Looking beamish, he took several small nibbles of his tea cake. Glancing down at the letter and pausing between bites, he went on in a low, gossipy tone: "More good news, my dears. They are going to advance my first month's salary, and I have decided to buy each of you a sweet or meat, any delicacy you'd favor for a feast!"

"A feast?" Grandmother's eyes brightened. "Quite generous of you, Horace. Are you sure?" Grandmother asked, her cheeks blossoming with color.

"But of course. It is ever so important to do something special for all of you, ever so important to celebrate my fortuitous rise."

"A feast would be a bright spot. Most welcome," Rose said.

"Oysters on the half shell with drawn butter and fresh lemon, to begin with," Horace said.

There was a murmur of approval.

"Pheasant with wild rice and chestnut dressing for the main course," Rose said, smacking her lips.

"Would a Nesselrode pudding be too much?" Grandmother asked.

"It would be like old times, Hortensia," Rose said, dabbing at her eyes with a tea napkin.

"Like old times," Grandmother echoed with a far-away look.

Horace swallowed a great bit of cake, downed with a gulp of tea. "I propose Hattie accompany me on Saturday, a grand outing to shop for the feast."

"Please, Grandmother," I said. I might catch sight of my classmates—or rather, they might catch sight of me with Horace. They would be impressed by Horace, who was always gallant and charming to everyone, but to ladies and girls in particular. Tomorrow, I could tell Aggie and Effie about the feast. Something true. Not straw nothings spun into golden lies.

That night I retrieved Grandfather's little book and studied it in the cheerless cold of my room. The second floor was poorly heated; I hunched in a wool coverlet, using the lamp to warm my face and fingers and to see the tiny printed letters clearly. Grandfather had written out rows of letters with no spaces to show where words began and ended.

Horace had taught me about da Vinci, a brilliant Italian who had lived centuries before me. He'd painted the *Mona Lisa* for one thing, but he had also written backward and from right to left in his many notebooks. His writing was easy enough to decipher if you held it up to a mirror, though it wasn't at all easy for people in his time to do that or even realize what he was doing, because most people didn't have mirrors and even if they had, most of them couldn't read or write. It was worth a try.

Taking the lamp from its stand by the bed, I set it on my bureau and held the open book in front of the lamp so the pages reflected in the mirror. I was right. Held to the mirror, the letters righted themselves. But they still didn't spell any words.

The kerosene lamp started to smoke and blacken its chimney. I turned down the wick, slipped the book under my pillow, and snuggled into bed. I had the sweet feeling that I would figure out Grandfather's secret message real soon. I would discover the lost fortune and then Grandmother's old life would be real again, and my fairy-tale lies would be true. I would save us.

Chapter Eight

When I got to school, Aggie wasn't there yet. None of the girls were. Miss Finster was standing at the front of the room like a gray cloud. She was holding a sheet of paper so close to her face that it could be touching her nose. She must have heard the clatter of my boots on the oiled wood floor. Startled, she quickly dropped the paper onto her desk. "Lettie," she said with her usual squinty scowl, "you're early."

I sucked in my breath. Poor Miss Finster had poor eyesight. That was why she'd gotten my name wrong. That was why she squinted so much and had held the paper so close to her face. I walked slowly up to her desk. "Hattie," I corrected gently. "My first name is Hattie."

"Hattie?" Her eyes widened. "Of course, Hattie. What was I thinking?" She laughed in an embarrassed sort of way. "Yes, Miss Finster sees that now." She drew her eyebrows together. "Boys and girls come and go as quickly as trolley cars here. Hard to keep you all straight."

"Yes, ma'am," I said. Miss Finster was a good sort. A bit befuddled, but the scowling was not about sternness at all. My heartbeat slowed but thudded sharply again as Aggie and Effie and the others filed into the room. Aggie and Effie came right up to stand by me.

"Miss Finster, may I change seats and sit near Hattie?" Aggie asked.

"I'm not changing with you," Effie said quickly, flashing me a quiet smile.

"Good of you to make friends with our new girl, Agnes. So quickly, too," Miss Finster cooed.

"Please, Miss Finster? Pretty please?" Aggie pleaded.

The teacher studied Aggie. "Hattie's work must be monitored," she said. "But you may switch seats with her and sit across from Effie."

"Hattie's smart. She doesn't need any help," Aggie said.

41

"I'm sorry, Agnes," Miss Finster said. "Miss Finster is firm about this. You must obey the teacher," she said sternly.

"We can still be friends at recess and lunch," I said. I linked one arm with her and one with Effie. My heart swelled with warmth for girls who fought to be with me, sit with me.

But at recess, Miss Finster asked me to stay in with her. "What have you studied exactly?" she asked as soon as the room was clear.

I ticked off the list for her on my fingers: "Art, languages, literature, philosophy, social studies, geography, history, writing, and recitation. And algebra, a little."

"My, my. You have gone beyond us. What to do?" Miss Finster said thoughtfully. "Greek comes on the secondary level at the Academy, and algebra isn't taught until grade eight. Didn't your tutor know that?" She clicked her tongue. Then she brightened. "Miss Finster will make an exception here and continue with algebra. Good minds need good challenges."

I got a good warm feeling. "Thank you, Miss Finster," I said.

"Good. Very good. It's all settled then. It is, isn't it,

Hat-tee?" she said, pronouncing my name carefully and looking pleased with herself.

"Yes, thank you," I said. I was pleased with her, too.

"Fine then," she said. "We're glad things are going well for you here and that you're fitting in with the other girls."

"Yes, ma'am." I swallowed and looked down. I wasn't really fitting in; I was showing off, but it was fun. The girls liked it. They wanted it.

At lunch, I slipped back to squeeze in next to Aggie and across from Effie. They had both brought clean hankies and were using them as napkins. Generously, I traded my lunch, and let them use my silver fork and china saucer. And I told them about our feast, but I didn't stop there. Words tumbled out of my mouth like a necklace of pearls. And why not? It would all be true soon enough, as soon as I found the hidden treasure. I told them about the cook, and added a but-ler, upstairs maids, and downstairs maids. I stopped. It wasn't much of a lie. Nothing huge really. We did have a cook, after all.

"Tell us more," Effie begged, making quiet little claps with her hands.

I swallowed. I had told everything I could think of, but Effie was so eager, like a baby bird chirping for worms. Wildly, I thought about what else I could add. I might embellish the way Horace often did . . . for fun. It wasn't ever expected that I believe him. It was just for fun. So, I told them about Grandmother's chandelier, with crystal prisms that cried rainbows; about our best slippers, with diamond buckles that sparkled like hundreds of stars; and about my best gown, with rubies and emeralds sewn into the bodice. Effie gobbled up my words like French bonbons, and I felt only a little guilty.

"It's just like a fairy tale come to life," Effie said. "Think of it . . . a chandelier that cries rainbows," she whispered.

Aggie listened real close. But she didn't say anything.

After school, Effie and Aggie walked toward the hill with me. The three of us skipped a ways, our arms around each other's waists just like we'd been friends forever. When it was time for me to start up the hill, Aggie said, "Why are you living with your grandmother, Hattie?"

"It's only temporary," I said. I swallowed. I didn't

want to tell them the truth, but I didn't want to lie, either. I was stuck.

"Are your folks traveling abroad?" Effie asked.

I nodded slowly. They didn't need to know about the cabin and the dirt floor. Or Pa, who could barely read and write. Or that Ma was dead, which was hard for me to tell.

"They don't work at all?" Aggie asked, looking shocked.

A sick feeling started in my stomach and left a bitter taste in my mouth, making me just want to heave it all up, get the true facts right out of me, especially when I thought about Pa, who worked harder than anybody. I swallowed really hard. "They're . . . they're . . ." I searched for something to say. I didn't know much more than a thimbleful about rich people, so I said what came to mind first, blurting it out in a rush: "They're settling Grandfather's estate in . . . in England. The Greymoors."

"Greymoors. It sounds so rich," Effie said happily. "I have a rich friend."

I left them and started up the hill to Grandmother's, feeling worse than wicked about my lies. Pretty near everything that had come out of my mouth today had been a lie. I hadn't planned it that way, but I liked spinning straw into the gold of a fairy tale. Effie and Aggie liked it, too, and that's the way it had to be from now on. But the part about Pa not working, that was different. Different from anything I'd ever done. And worse.

When I was in front of Ivy's house, I knew someone was watching me. But when I glanced up, whoever it was stepped away from the window and let the curtain fall. When I stepped inside Grandmother's house, the hall mirror and my guilty reflection were waiting for me.

Chapter Nine

Saturday morning, Horace and I set off with a shopping list and a basket. A soft, powdery snow had fallen overnight and covered up the piles of coal ash and sooty snow along the walks. Already the avenue was filling with horse-drawn sleighs and the merry jingling of bells in the crisp, cold air. The sun on my face was warm, and I skipped a little beside Horace, who was always easy to be with.

"Let's walk down and take the trolley back," Horace said. "We'll drool over the pastries and chocolates, the baubles and trinkets in the shop windows. You haven't said, Hattie, but I insist that you choose a delicacy for the feast."

"Hmm . . . not raisins, onions, cabbage, fish, oatmeal, soft-boiled eggs. . . . You know better than anyone," I said. I looked around, hoping I would spy one of the girls from school.

"I do," Horace said. We had reached Broadway, and now there was traffic everywhere, delivery wagons, sleighs darting and speeding through cross streets. Trolley wheels whined. Smoke from chimneys and clouds scudded overhead in a winter-blue sky. Talking became nearly impossible, but Horace and I strolled along, threading through crowds of shoppers on foot, vendors, and delivery men.

"Look, Horace, at the window over there," I said, tugging on his arm.

"Where? Windows are everywhere."

Even though pointing was impolite and forbidden by Grandmother, I pointed. "Across the street. *Wadsworth Stationery and Books,*" I read aloud. The window was ablaze with color, decorated with red and white lace hearts and cupids. "Saint Valentine's," I said in wonder. "Might we go in, Horace. Please?" I tingled with possibility. I could make valentines for all the girls. They would love it. Perfect for a princess in a fairy tale.

"Ah, a book, of course," Horace said, winking as he

crooked his arm for me. "It is a stunning sight, a feast of another sort," he said as we walked across the street, mindful of speeding sleighs and steaming horse droppings.

"Valentines," I said. "Please?"

"It's the least I can do," Horace said. "I suspect I will be eating your fair share of oysters."

"Oysters, ugh," I said with a shudder.

"Precisely," Horace said. He bent himself nearly in two and whispered in my ear, "Valentines are a lovely choice. Very thoughtful, Hattie. I quite approve."

"Oh, Horace, thank you," I whispered back. Delighted, I stepped inside. How hard it was to choose—lace hearts were a must, and I needed enough sheets of scrap-paper flowers to make valentines for the girls and Miss Finster, the old ones, and Horace. I added a small tablet for deciphering the code in Grandfather's *Treasure* book.

By the time we finished shopping, Horace and I were laden down with packages, footsore, and happily exhausted. The trolley car was welcome even with coal ashes and mud, slushy snow tracked on by passengers, and the tobacco spittle and butts of discarded cigars that littered the floor. I clutched my parcel with my new tablet and the lace papers for making valentines. All thanks to Horace.

"I do hope we haven't forgotten anything," Horace said. He pulled the list from his coat pocket. "Nesselrode pudding. Delicious no doubt, but enough ingredients to open a grocer's." He studied the list again, and by now the trolley had reached the last stop at the top of Broadway and we set out for home.

When we were close, I looked down the avenue toward Grandmother's. Even from this distance, today the great house had a gray pallor of winter like a shadow of the bright blue from the Vandermeers' house next door.

When we reached the Vandermeers', a sleigh and horses came up the drive from the stable barn and stopped at the end of the walk. The butler flung open the front door of the house, and Ivy Victoria came out and down the steps. She was dressed in a burgundy velvet coat trimmed with white fur, her yellow hair flowing over her shoulders. Scowling and spouting, her mother came behind her dressed in the indigo velvet of a wrathful thundercloud. "Be careful! Be careful!" she was shouting.

Surprisingly, Horace made no amusing comment; he didn't seem to notice at all. He just stared straight ahead, lost in a fog. But Ivy noticed us. She looked our way, right at me.

My stomach fluttered. I wasn't sure what to do. I felt frozen like an ice statue. But Ivy didn't look scared or unfriendly. I lifted one barely thawed hand in a half wave, stiff-like. If she ignored it, I could keep bringing my arm up to brush hair away from my face.

She blinked in surprise and looked quickly over her shoulder before taking the hand of the driver and climbing into the sleigh. Her mother, wheezing and panting from the effort of moving, struggled with the step up into the sleigh even with the help of the driver.

But when Horace and I walked past the entrance to the drive, Ivy Victoria stood up in the sleigh and waved, a secret wave, her hand close to her face so her mother wouldn't see. I waved again. I didn't know if we could be friends or not. Probably not. But that wave was something. Something real. Something that made me think that Ivy Victoria did want to be my friend, even if her mother didn't approve. It was enough to make me add Ivy Victoria to my list for a valentine.

Chapter Ten

Horace was still in a fog when we climbed the steps at Grandmother's. It was so unlike him not to be giddy over a feast. I jiggled his arm. "Horace, are you all right?" I asked.

"Hattie, you are a dear to care so much. I'm fine, really. Just tired. So much to do before Monday," he said wearily.

"Cheer up, Horace. You don't have to do everything. Rose wouldn't hear of it," I chided as we hung our coats and removed our galoshes. Then we set off for the kitchen, where Grandmother and Rose fell on us.

Almost at once, Horace seemed to brighten up. "For the feast," he announced, and made a spirited show of displaying each special ingredient as if it were a precious gem. The old ones twittered like birds, not noticing that Horace's smoky eyes looked troubled.

Still clutching my parcel, I wanted to run up to my room to work on solving the code. But I couldn't. How could I possibly leave Horace? But it was Horace who rescued me.

"Off with you, Hattie," Horace said, making shooing motions. "You do have plans for the afternoon, I believe. Things to make?"

Biting my lip, I nodded furiously. Valentine's was fast-approaching, so it made a perfect excuse for me to work on secret, special cards in my room.

"Plans? What things?" Grandmother said. "Whatever it is can wait, I should think." There was a definite scold in her voice. Gentle but firm.

"Too many cooks . . ." Horace began.

"Too many?" Rose said. "There's plenty of work to go around and only one cook as far as I can tell."

Horace raised his eyebrows and winked broadly. "Hattie has her own special work, and what sort of cook's helper has she ever been?"

"Hattie does a great many things very well," Grandmother said, sounding perturbed.

"I'll wash up," I promised.

Rose gave a snappy glance from my brown parcel to my face. Her eyes lit. She'd guessed about the valentines. "Washing up is plenty enough. More than," she said.

"Oh, dear, of course. Whatever was I thinking?" Grandmother said, finally catching on.

I gave Grandmother a swift hug and hurried away. I fairly flew up the stairs. My fingers shook as I untied the knotted string of the parcel. I admired the beautiful red and white lace, but I quickly grabbed up my new tablet and began copying from the first page of Grandfather's book, hoping to discover a secret message that would lead to the lost fortune.

First I wrote the letters backward, exactly as Grandfather had written them down. Underneath, I wrote the letters in the usual way. I already knew that the mirror trick wouldn't magically produce words that I could read, so I knew that if it was secret writing, it would need more deciphering than da Vinci's.

By the time I was done, my brain and eyes both wanted to go crossed. I sat back and gave my effort a long study:

ꞁꞇꞇᴉbooʞonuuɯlоʞоʇɥʇ
thtokmnnokoodittrf

But try as I might, Grandfather's nonsense writing made no sense. Momentarily defeated, I closed Grandfather's book, hid it under my pillow again, and set to work on valentines. I knew I'd better start just in case someone came up to check on me. They always checked on me. I spread the paper lace and the scrap-paper flowers that Horace had bought on my bed. I wanted to say just the right thing on each valentine. I decided to start with the hardest ones first. I sighed and flipped to a clean page on my new tablet.

To Ivy Victoria

On Valentine's Day
I wanted to say
Sorry for the way
I threatened to scalp you.
What I said wasn't true,
But what else could I do
When you said that my grandfather
Was murdered and buried in
Our garden?

I thought it was pretty good except for the end. Then I read it out loud. On second thought, I decided it was horrible in general and that it was risky to remind her of the scary details. She'd been pretty horrible to me too, but I was sure her mother had put her up to it. I flipped over to the next page and tried again.

POEM TO IVY VICTORIA VANDERMEER

Please forgive me if I say
That I'm sorry on this day
For all the mean things that I said.
If we cannot be friends, then let us be kindly neighbors.
HAPPY SAINT VALENTINE'S DAY

- Hattie Belle Basket -

Better, but still not very poetic. I crossed out all the lines except the last two. I was hopeless when it came to poetry. I sighed again and flipped to a clean page. This time I decided to try writing one for Effie and Aggie. I wanted to be especially kind and sweet. I thought and thought, but I couldn't think of anything princess-perfect to write.

I was about to go back to Grandfather's book again, when a *tap, tap* sounded on my door. The knob turned and Horace poked his head in. "How's it going, old girl?" he asked.

"Not too well," I said. "No soul of a poet here."

He opened the door wider. He didn't look melancholy like before, but he still wasn't his usual self. More like a washed-out string from a mop head. No sparkle. No sign that a great feast was in the making. "Maybe I can help," he said.

I shook my head. "It's something I have to do myself. I'm just not very good at it."

"How about variations on the tried-and-true theme of *Roses are red, violets are blue*?"

I brightened. "I can do that. Short, flowery, sweet. Perfect," I said, sliding off the bed. "Thanks, Horace. What about you? Can I help you?"

"Help me with what?" he asked, looking puzzled.

I shook my head. "I was just trying to be a friend."

"You are a dear friend. I'm your friend, too," he said, softening. "You do know that, right, Hattie?"

"Horace, of course I do." I looked down, bewildered by how intense he sounded. What was bothering him?

"It's the hour to dine. That's what I came up to

tell you." Horace turned. "After the great feast tomorrow, I'm . . ."

"I'm stuck with the washing up," I said, hoping he would offer to help me. But he didn't.

"Oh . . . right," was all he said. Together we walked down the stairs in silence.

Chapter Eleven

Saturday after dinner, I was not excused to go to my room to work. There were still too many preparations to do before the feast. Grandmother and I were to polish the silver; Horace and Rose were to put the final touches on the Nesselrode pudding and make the chestnut stuffing. No chance for me to decipher the code before tomorrow. No chance of presenting Grandmother with the lost fortune at the feast. Surprisingly, I was only a little dismayed. Maybe because tonight it was comforting just to see the old ones humming over their work like happy bees over flowers—something that I hadn't seen since Grandfather died. How good and generous of Horace to think of making a feast for us.

On Sunday, we all did our part helping Rose in the kitchen, setting and serving, eating and clearing, making room for the next course. The feast was lovely. Smashing, really. I tried a bit of everything, even putting down an oyster on the half shell smothered with butter. I gagged only a little and covered it up by coughing in my hand. At least none of them raised an eyebrow or looked down their nose.

The pheasant and chestnut stuffing, however, made the feast. "Succulent. Piquant herbs. Lovely nutty flavor," I said, stealing verbiage from Horace's past remarks before he had a chance to use the words himself. I ate my own good share. More, maybe, which surprised everyone. Gaily I thought of the things I would say to Aggie and Effie.

"Well, I never," Rose said in wonder, looking most pleased. "It's a rare day indeed."

"Indeed," Grandmother echoed, looking proud.

But then came Grandmother's favored Nesselrode pudding. There were hard little pieces of fruit that tasted oddly not like fruit, and the plump, swollen raisins that always made me think of flies, black bugs, or rat leavings. I swallowed a few bites whole under Grandmother's watchful eye and tried not to make a shuddery face.

"Exquisite," Horace said of the pudding. "Simply divine, Madame Rose. An excellent choice, Madame Greymoor." Horace's jolliness was forced, but the old ones didn't seem to notice the troubled look in his eyes. Thoughtfully, I pushed my serving over to him.

But no sooner was the pudding eaten than a most curious thing happened. With a melancholy sigh, Horace pushed back his chair, got up from the table, and slouched from the room. We heard his tread go lightly up the stairs.

"I can't think . . . what do you suppose?" Grandmother said.

"Hmpf . . . obvious, I should say," Rose said. "For once, Hattie didn't give him the greater share of her meal. You did stuff yourself with pheasant," Rose said to me.

"Hattie feeds him quite too much of her meals. Quite too much," Grandmother sputtered. "But, in truth, Rose, you did make quite the do about Hattie having seconds."

I said nothing. For a few minutes, reflective silence hung over the table. I knew Horace didn't care if I ate my fair share. Deep inside, I knew it wasn't about food at all. I knew it, because I had seen it in his face. But what *was* it about?

Rose cast me a dark, buzzardy look as if I did know something but wasn't telling. "Washing-up time," she snapped.

Feeling sorry for myself, I picked up my plate and Horace's and went to the kitchen. I got busy making noise, banging and clanging pots and cooking dishes, getting everything in order for washing. In no time at all, Grandmother and Rose came in with glasses and silver and plates. Grandmother went back to finish clearing, and Rose grabbed up a linen towel and began to dry. Nobody spoke for a long time. The kitchen trembled with clattering dishes, sloshing dishwater, and Rose huffing grumpily next to me.

"If you know something, you'd better spit it out," Rose said crossly.

"Know as much as you," I said.

"Move over," she ordered me now. "A good cook does her own dishes. I'll wash; you dry." Which suited both of us better. At least, it did me.

Things simmered down after that, and we settled into doing our jobs, but not for long. I could feel Rose thinking by her furious scrubbing. I just kept wiping plates and silverware and minding my own business, which meant keeping my mouth shut.

I sighed. "Rose, it's nothing to do with us. How could it? Horace is ever so dear to us."

"And you are my dearest hearts," Horace said. He came in as if nothing had been amiss before and went to warm his hands by the range.

Horace's coming in suddenly that way made Rose drop a plate into the water, giving both of us a good soaking.

"It's cold as the grave up there," Horace said. "The heart of the house, and all the warmth, is right here." But there was a faint breath of sadness in his voice.

"It is," said Rose with emotion. The kitchen was her kingdom.

Wiping the last of the dishes, I turned to lean against the sink and study him. "It is lovely here . . . safe," I said. Then Grandmother came in, and we settled down together by the stove for tea with honey and lemon.

"Quite the dunce I was at dinner," Horace said quietly, his head bent over his steaming cup. "Didn't mean to alarm. Agitated a bit, you know. Jitters over the new job. Quite a lot riding on my future."

Yes, that made good sense. New things meant new worries.

As Horace stumbled on, the troubled look eased out

of the old ones' faces. But then he drew in a long, deep, shuddery breath. "I wanted to tell you right away, on Friday, after the meeting at the Academy," he said. "But it came as a shock to me, so sudden and so painful to tell you, but now I must, because . . . because I'm . . . I'm leaving."

Horace took a gulp of tea and then plunged on. "I'm asked to take up residence . . . in charge of boys on the first level. Nothing to say about it really, just part of the duties required of me. I'm expected. One or two days to get my things together and move to the boarding house. I'll visit when I can get free." But by the way he said that, it meant he probably couldn't get free at all. He looked horribly woebegone. Big dollops of tears popped out of his eyes.

Grandmother and Rose had the look of winter on their faces. But they rallied round Horace, patting and shushing and offering kind words that they couldn't possibly mean. They told him it was fine. They said they understood. They said he had to make his own way and they were proud that he had gotten a leg up in the world.

But it wasn't fine. My mouth went dry, and a pang of sadness squeezed my heart when I thought of Horace no longer being here for afternoon tea in the library.

We would miss his laughter, his dramatic readings, his thoughtful understanding. He was like a brother, the very dearest sort. What would we do without his good heart and cheer to fill the house and jolly us along through the hard times?

The house was tomblike all evening, as if a spell had been cast over the house and we had been rendered speechless. But I couldn't dwell on Horace. I had work to do. I still had Grandfather's secret book and a fortune to find.

That night I studied all the letters I'd copied in my tablet from Grandfather's book. I studied them for a long time, thinking they would work themselves out in my head, the way the answers to story problems did without my having to write down all the steps in the formula.

I was close to deciphering it. I could feel it happening. I needed it to happen, but it didn't happen right then.

Chapter Twelve

A few nights later, after a very tearful supper, Horace left for his new lodgings. I missed him at breakfast. I missed his whistling and his cheerful, "Good morning, madames and mademoiselle." I missed him eating the plump raisins in my oatmeal for me. Horace's pleasure over every little thing made all of us appreciate things more, too. There was just so much to miss about Horace. The house was like an empty coat without him.

This morning I wasn't hungry at all. This morning we were all picky eaters. Now that Horace had left, Rose wore her dark, buzzardy scowl again, and Grandmother worried her lace collar the way she had before December 26, when the news came about

Grandfather. I wanted to blurt out that things would soon be better. But I didn't. I had an uneasy feeling in my stomach, a rumble taunting me that I was never going to solve the secret code.

I had to find the fortune. Everything would be better then, even better than before. When I did find it, Horace would come back. He wouldn't have to work anymore. He could sketch fashions and write poetry, go to the opera and theater. Grandmother would have servants again to do all the work, and Rose could take her ease, if she wanted to. I could have parties like Ivy Victoria's, with costumes, confections, and conundrums. It would be soon.

I wanted to tell Effie and Aggie about the code book, but I knew I'd better wait until the treasure was a true fact. Besides, they already thought our life on the hill was all luxury now. But what else could I tell them that wasn't too false? At recess, when we were walking around the school grounds arm in arm, it came to me what I could say. I took a bit of straw and began to spin.

"The seamstress is coming soon," I said. It sounded true. After all, we were almost like seamstresses ourselves. We had done lots of altering and sewing. I had helped. A little. "She brings bolts of material, laces from

Belgium, fabric from France, ribbons and buttons. She stays for a long time," I said, borrowing what I knew from spying on the doings at Ivy's and what I'd learned from Horace's designing fashions for me from my mother's old gowns. All of us had helped with the cutting and pinning, the fitting and sewing. "Grandmother said I am to have a new velvet dress and a velvet coat trimmed with real fur, a velvet bonnet, and a real fur muff to keep my hands warm. A Kate Greenaway dress if I want."

"Will you wear them to school?" Effie asked.

I shook my head. "Grandmother said they are for special occasions like winter parties."

"You might at least show us," Aggie said, sounding miffed. "You might invite us to one of your parties."

I wet my lips, swallowed. "I'd like to, but Grandmother is in mourning," I said, looking momentarily sorrowful. "I'm not allowed to have parties yet."

"Maybe you don't think we're good enough for Snob Hill," Aggie said.

My heart went stone cold for a second. Spinning a fairy tale was fragile work. "Aggie," I said, "you and Effie are my truest friends. You will be the first ones I invite."

"Promise?" Effie said.

"Promise," I said. And even Aggie seemed satisfied with that, though she didn't accept things as easily as Effie did.

After school, I hurried right home, not caring whether Ivy was watching for me. I wasn't worried about the tax letter behind the mirror, not even worried about what might have come in the mail. I was going to work on the code until I solved it. I was no quitter, and I would prove it. Soon we would be wealthy. I'd have costume parties and prove to Aggie and Effie that I was their true friend.

I rushed in to see Grandmother and Rose in the kitchen getting tea things ready. Without Horace to join in and jolly them up, regale them with stories of town or school, their movements seemed slow, halfhearted. The dullness of their day showed on their faces, but I couldn't stop to cheer them; every minute was precious now.

"Please, may I work on something in my room?" I asked. They exchanged secretive, knowing looks. Grandmother nodded her assent, and off I went. I decided I'd better make a valentine to leave in plain sight before going down for tea.

But first I was going to have another go at Grandfather's secret writing. After several poor attempts to decipher, I got frustrated and turned the page. I would make Rose's valentine first, I decided.

FOR ROSE

Roses are red
Violets are blue
Sugar is sweet

But then I got stuck, because calling Rose sweet was a lie. Rose would know it; we all would. Actually, her peppery self was sort of fun. And then it struck me what would please her.

FOR MY GRAND-AUNT ROSE

Violets are purple; roses are pink.
You are the greatest cook
in the world, I think.
Happy Valentine's Day.

Love, Hattie Belle

Perfect. In the center of a lace heart, I pasted a flowery scrap of paper especially made for greetings, and carefully penned my message to Rose. I sat back and admired it. Rose was like an old aunt. She was almost like another grandmother. There. Pleased, I displayed Rose's valentine on my bureau. It reflected nicely in the mirror. After that, I wrote the sweetest poem for Grandmother, with lots of love in it, and one for Horace. I decided I should finish the valentines once and for all, with a sweet poem of friendship for Aggie and Effie, Miss Finster, and Ivy Victoria.

Then I got back to work on Grandfather's secret writing.

It was cold working in my room after the sun went down, which came not long after I got home from school. On the windows, the frost melted in the day, then turned to ice, nearly covering the entire pane of glass, but the hissing sound of the gaslights on the wall made a warm, pleasant sound and the kerosene lamp by my bed was a good place to warm my fingers.

While I worked, I wondered where the fortune would be, if the treasure would be rubies, diamonds, and emeralds, or large denominations of silver certificates. When I was still dreaming of treasure, a golden ray of afternoon sun slanted across the page, and I broke the code.

It's funny how when you set your mind to something, decide that you're going to do it, things just seem to come like magic. I didn't think it was magic, but it sort of felt that way.

First I transcribed the letters so they faced in the right direction, then turned them so that the letters that had been last were now first. Like this:

f r t t i d o o k o n n m k o t h t
i s i r e t l o d w a d a e u w a

While I was studying the letters, my left eye did a funny sort of shift. I could feel it in my eye and in my head, and there it was. The pattern fell into place. Grandfather had zigzagged the letters. He began at the top letter and dropped down to the second line to write the next letter in a word. Like this:

$$f_i r_s t$$

I wrote it out:

firstitriedtolookdownandmakeoutwhat

And again:

First I tried to look down and make out what . . .

Voilà! as Horace would say. My scalp and fingers tingled. My heart sang. I'd done it. I leafed through Grandfather's book. There were quite a few pages, and the printing was small. I'd have to work hard to get through it before Valentine's Day.

I bent over the page and began working some more. It came faster and faster, and soon I was speeding along. This is what appeared under my fingertips as I wrote:

Suddenly I came upon a little three-legged table, all made of solid glass; there was nothing on it except a tiny golden key, and my first thought was that it might belong to one of the doors of the hall; but, alas! Either the locks were too large, or the key was too small, but at any rate it would not open any of them.

That might be a clue to do with keys. Grandfather may have taken the clock keys to try in the locked doors.

But I could see no riddle, no treasure map of words at all. I needed more to go on.

How queer everything is today! And yesterday things went on just as usual. I wonder if I've been changed in the night? Let me think: was I the same when I got up this morning? I almost think I can remember feeling a little different.

If it was meant as a conundrum, it was a very odd one indeed. Agitated, I got up and went to the window that looked out on the Vandermeers'. I knelt on the cushion in the window seat and tried to scratch a hole in the icy frost, but it was much too thick. I pressed my lips against the corner pane and blew.

Through the small hole in the ice, I saw Ivy in her fur-trimmed velvet, her soft yellow ringlets swinging around her shoulders as she ran out to meet her father just coming through the black iron gate. I watched as her father bent down to hug her. I saw her sweet, silly look of joy. And felt a familiar pang.

I thought about my pa, about the shabby way I had lied to Aggie and Effie. "I'm not really ashamed of you, Pa," I whispered. How good it would be to have him coming home to me. He'd whistle like a hawk, probably catch me up in his strong arms, swing me around. I'd be just as silly with joy as Ivy was.

I began to shiver from the cold and went to warm my face and fingers near the lamp before going back to work. I flipped to the next page in Grandfather's book and began to write his words over in my tablet.

What a funny watch! It tells the day of the month, and doesn't tell what o'clock it is! Why should it?

I think you might do something better with the time than waste it in asking riddles that have no answers. If you knew Time as well as I do, you wouldn't talk about wasting it.

It is always six o'clock now. It's always teatime, and we've no time to wash the things between whiles.

This time, something about it struck me, reminded me of something I knew or almost knew. But what? I read back over all the words I had transcribed, and then it hit me. The words were from a book I had read in Grandmother's library. I gasped. It was a book with a loving inscription to my mother from Grandfather that mentioned conundrums and treasure. Perhaps the book was the key that would lead to the fortune! It was a clue in wide-open sight. I sat back against the bed. I felt very close to the answer.

As soon as dinner was over and the dishes done, I retrieved *Alice's Adventures in Wonderland*. It was on the bottom shelf of the bookcase near the window where all my mother's old books were kept. I slipped it from the shelf and went up the stairs to bed.

I was right; Grandfather had copied the words from *Alice's Adventures*. I read the book straight through to the end, but there was nothing I could make out that led to a new clue and the treasure. I still had several pages of the secret message to decipher and then I would know. But the kerosene in the lamp sputtered, and the flame went out. Vexed, I pounded my fists on the bedclothes and silently screamed.

I was so close, but I had no choice now but to wait. I took a slow, deep breath to calm myself. It would be okay. I would figure it out in no time, right after school tomorrow—on Valentine's Day. Perfect for a fairy-tale princess.

Chapter Thirteen

The next morning when I set the table for breakfast, I put the valentines for Grandmother and Rose by their place settings. They acted surprised in the spirit of the holiday but exchanged knowing glances. Rose was overcome with emotion when she read the verse I'd written. "'Grand-Aunt,' it says, Hortensia," Rose said, looking at me with true fondness.

"Our dear little mouse," Grandmother said proudly, using a special term of affection that she had used for my mother, too. The glow in the room would surely melt the frost and ice on the window sooner than the sun outside would. It was a good start to Valentine's Day, and this was just the beginning.

After breakfast, I rushed back to my room to get the rest of the valentines. I put the one for Horace aside and hoped that he'd come to visit soon. I looked at Ivy's. I picked it up and my heart started to pound. I put it down as if it were hot. Maybe it was too soon. Maybe I should wait another day. No. Do it now.

Feeling the glow of the day, I ran up the walk to Ivy Victoria's and slipped the valentine through the shiny brass letter slot. It clanged cheerily, and off I went to school with the rest of my precious valentines pressed against my cloak.

I was early. Happily, I placed a valentine on Miss Finster's desk and handed Aggie and Effie their special cards as soon as they came in. I wanted them to know they were special. My special friends.

Effie, who was naturally sweet and ladylike, hugged me. She traced a finger over the red lace heart and whispered the poem I'd copied down.

"Nice," Aggie said, sort of grudgingly. She held her valentine in both hands and just stared. I couldn't tell if she liked it or not.

"It's a lovely valentine," Effie said, looking dewy-eyed. "We should have gotten something for you."

Aggie poked her with an elbow. "Why would Hattie care about valentines? She's got jewels."

I did care a little. I didn't think they'd have anything to give me, but it would have been nice to show Grandmother that I had friends at common school.

At recess, I decided it was time to plan a party. I would invite them soon, as soon as I found the treasure, but I would tell them now. Effie would love it. "I'm planning a small tea party," I said. "I know Grandmother will let me have one. And I want both of you to come. We'll have games and our dear cook, Rose, will make a hidden treasure cake." I had heard about it from Horace, and it sounded mysterious and enchanting. "There will be pastries and confections, a game of Secrets . . ." I sifted through my head for other things to add.

"Secrets?" Effie asked.

"Oh," I said. My mother had told me about them. "Bonbons, chocolate nuts, sugarplums twisted into shiny squares of colored paper with"—I lowered my voice — "a folded slip of paper with a conundrum written on it."

"Sort of like a story problem?" Aggie asked with a snort.

"No," I said. "The answer is written on it. You read the conundrum to see who can guess it first."

"Yup, story problem," Aggie said, but her eyes lit up like Secrets was something she'd like to do.

"I can't come to your party," Effie said. "I don't have a party dress." Her lower lip began to quiver.

"It doesn't matter," I said soothingly. "You can wear your school dresses. I just want you to come, because you're my friends," I said, feeling a little wilted.

"What about your other friends? Will they wear school dresses?" Aggie asked, fire snapping in her eyes. She tugged hard on the satin ribbons of my red dress, the claret wool that wasn't even my best. But the ribbons were sewn on tight and didn't rip off. "It does matter," she said coldly, "and you know it."

I bit my tongue and clasped my hands behind my back to keep from yanking her wild coppery hair. We went back to the schoolroom without talking. I swallowed my hurt and busied myself with story problems. Had I made them think that party gowns had emeralds and rubies, that party slippers had diamond buckles? The fairy-tale lies weren't fun anymore. Inside, I had a big, empty ache that had been full of friendship.

At the end of the day, the teacher handed me a note for Grandmother. She must have seen the alarmed look on my face, because she gently touched my hand. "It's nothing to worry about, Hattie," she said with a smile of shared conspiracy. "Miss Finster thinks that your grandmother will be delighted."

After school, Effie gave me a shy smile, but she went off with Aggie, and I walked home alone. I understood about not belonging, about having the wrong clothes and the wrong way of talking, but how could I make them understand that I knew what it was like? My throat was swollen with tears, and now I was almost afraid to look up at Ivy's. But I did. Ivy was at the window, holding back the curtain. She smiled and waved. A real wave, not a secret, hiding-from-her-mother wave.

I waved back and smiled. The ache eased a little. Ivy knew the truth about me, about Pa. She knew all the gossip about my family, but there she was, smiling. Not a made-up smile, but a real smile. I waved again, then headed up the walk to Grandmother's house.

I opened the door and looked down to see if there

was any mail. A pile of valentines rested inside like a snowdrift. One to Grandmother, one to Rose, and one to me from dear Horace. He hadn't forgotten us after all. And there was one from Ivy. A lovely burgundy heart that felt like velvet. Slowly, my heart fluttering like little bird wings, I whispered the words of the verse:

HAPPY VALENTINE'S DAY TO HATTIE BELLE BASKET

When evening draws her curtains
And pins them with a star,
Remember I am your true friend,
No matter where you are.
Forget me not—

- Ivy Victoria Vandermeer -

I hugged the velvety card to my chest. Ivy wanted a true friend as much as I did. She wanted me to be her friend. She really did. The valentine verse said so.

And then I saw it. On the bottom of the pile. Another envelope from the tax collector. This time FINAL NOTICE was stamped on it in bold red letters. My heart skipped from happiness to fear in a single beat. I breathed in and out fast, trying to catch my breath. I didn't know much about tax collection, but I knew that FINAL NOTICE was a very bad thing.

I looked up from studying the envelope, straight into my own eyes. I saw myself as clear as anything in the hall mirror. I gulped. "Mirror, mirror, on the wall, who's the guiltiest one of all?" I whispered.

I stared down at the envelope in my hands. I knew I should take it straight to Grandmother. I should. But I didn't. I stuck it underneath my valentines. I swallowed hard. Maybe it wouldn't matter at all in a little while. I crossed my fingers and hoped that Grandfather's secret message would lead to the fortune. I would find it tonight.

Chapter Fourteen

I was greeted by the strong odors of cabbage and ham as I started down the hall. I knew it was a boiled ham dinner tonight, with ugly vegetables—cabbage and rutabaga, turnips and carrots—that gave me squeamish shudders when they touched my tongue. The fluffy dumplings and the ham were all I could tolerate properly, and with Horace gone, the boiled dinner would last the rest of the week.

When I poked my head into the library, Grandmother was bent over Grandfather's soft wool suit. She was ripping out seams. She looked so small and frail, like a china doll. "Grandmother," I called softly, "there're valentines come for you and Rose from Horace."

She looked up, her face brightening when she saw me. "What a dear boy. Rose will be so pleased that he hasn't forgotten us. Thank you, too, my little mouse. Your valentines made quite the bright spot for us all day."

I swallowed. The guilt of the hidden tax notice scorched my hand. "I'll set them here on the tea table," I said, putting the valentines down along with the note from Miss Finster and my lunch box. "I'll be in my room."

Grandmother glanced at the clock. "We dine in an hour. Why not sit here where it's warm, keep me company?" she said. But already she was glancing down at her work, her fingers nervously brushing the wool.

I nodded but turned and went quickly to my room all the same. She was busy and what I had to do couldn't wait. The bell would ring all too soon for me to go down and set the table and help serve.

I lit my lamp, grabbed up Grandfather's code book, and set right to work without removing my cloak. There were still three pages left. This time, as I decoded the lines, I recognized passages from *Alice*. Until the end. The very last page. This time it was different. At last. I heaved a sigh of welcome relief. It was a message to my mother.

Lily, dear: If you are reading these words, then you have deciphered my code and discovered the book. But have you found the treasure yet, my dear?

There was more, but I had to stop. I shivered with excitement. In a few more minutes . . . I took a deep breath, flipped the page of my tablet, and plunged on.

There is a treasure to be found at the end, at the very end. Down the rabbit hole, dear. Look beyond . . . beyond the end.

I looked up and pressed my lips together. Rabbit hole. Beyond the end. Whatever did he mean? I got up and went over to my bureau to get *Alice.* I read the inscription again.

To my beloved Lily at Christmas,
Mysteries aplenty and treasure too—that's what you'll find in these pages for you.
Abiding love from your father.

I leafed to the last page. To the end. Then beyond. I opened the book wide, bent the binding backward. I gasped. I saw the faint outline of something . . . something thin sheathed behind the endpaper.

The endpaper was a hidden pocket. My heart thudded, and shivers went up over my scalp and down my arms to my fingers. With tingling fingers, I eased the paper from its hiding place. *A treasure map?* I tingled all over now.

Slowly, I unfolded the paper. It was not a treasure map. It was a letter, a letter to my mother, to Lily.

Lily, dear: The treasure can be found by looking in the mirror. Mirror, mirror, on the wall, you are the dearest treasure of all. Love, Father

I read the letter again, slowly, letting the truth sink in. There was no treasure. No fortune to save us. None at all. Nothing. A hard lump swelled in my throat. My eyes burned. But it was true what he wrote. Ma was the dearest treasure of all. She was the sugar that had kept me sweet and mostly good. But I wasn't good anymore. I had lied to Grandmother and to Effie and Aggie. *Mirror, mirror, on the wall.* When I looked in Grandmother's mirror, all that reflected back was guilt and betrayal.

I let the paper flutter from my fingers and stared at

my empty hands. My heart thudded painfully. There was nothing else to be done. I had to tell Grandmother about the taxes. I had to give her the final notice. I had to tell Effie and Aggie there would be no party. No confections. No costumes. No conundrums.

Seized with sudden panic, I grabbed the book again. There had to be more. There must be. I slid my fingers into the endpaper again. There *was* more. My heartbeat quickened again. Maybe it was a clue, or it might be . . . It was. I could feel by the texture that it was paper money. *Please. Please. Please, let it be a silver certificate. A big one.* I closed my eyes and wished really hard, carefully inching it from its hiding place.

Slowly, I opened my eyes and looked at what was in my hand. It was paper money, as I had hoped, but it was green. One single dollar. Something, but not nearly enough. I swallowed the lump in my throat and blinked really, really hard. I glanced at the final notice. I had not saved us at all. I had made things worse.

The bell rang for me to come down and set the table. I picked up the envelope and Grandfather's book and got as far as the top of the stairs. But I ran back and shoved everything, including the dollar, under my pillow. It could wait a little longer. Why spoil Valentine's Day for the old ones?

I rushed down to set the table. Just as I finished, Rose stumped in with the soup tureen and placed it in the center of the table.

"It's been quite like old times, getting valentines," Grandmother said, taking her place at the table.

Rose nodded, her face softening. "Lily always made lovely cards. She always remembered her old cook. Now we've got Hattie and Horace."

"We are blessed," said Grandmother.

She and Rose looked at me with sweet affection, the sort no doubt they had always given my mother. But I wasn't good like my mother. Not gentle and sweet. Not even close. Not even when I tried.

"What a nice note from your teacher, Hattie, dear," Grandmother said now. "Quite proud of you, I'd say."

In all my woes and worries, I had forgotten about the note. "Miss Finster is kind," I said. "And . . . interesting."

"She's written with wonderful news," Grandmother twittered. "Horace should be here to hear this, since he deserves so much of the credit."

"He should be here anyway," Rose growled.

Grandmother went on, "Miss Finster writes that you are advanced beyond even the older grades. She recommends that you take the Regents exams, which are required for entrance to secondary school, at the end of this month." Grandmother lowered her voice. "She says that your advantages and circumstances are so different from the others." Grandmother looked at me as if finally I had risen to the class I was intended for—high society. "I quite approve," she said, looking peacock proud.

"Hattie will live here, of course, which settles the problem of board." She spoke now as if I weren't present. "Tuition is something I hadn't seen arising just yet. But our Hattie must have an advantageous start."

Rose was puffing, her face mottled. "Hortensia, how do you propose to pay for tuition? You've either nothing worth giving away or things too valuable to sell. You can't mean to part with your few remaining heirlooms?"

"Really, Rose, you do make quite too much about these matters. This is not the time to discuss it." Grandmother was unruffled, but she wouldn't be so dismissive about money if she knew about the tax notices. Once I gave them to her, she wouldn't be so calm. She would worry and fret about not having the money for tuition.

Once, I had believed that Grandmother needed me around to love her. But she was so devoted to me that she would sacrifice her treasured heirlooms, even go without eating to pay my tuition. I couldn't let her do that. But if I wasn't here . . . If I left, Grandmother wouldn't have to worry about the Academy and tuition anymore. If I wasn't here, things would be altogether easier for her. She wouldn't have to worry about feeding me or heating extra rooms either. Grandmother would miss me, but she would be better off without me.

Right then and there, I decided I should leave, run away. I'd go to Pa. I would do it tomorrow.

Chapter Fifteen

At breakfast, a sick feeling was rising and spreading as fast as floodwater inside me. In my rush to finish eating, I choked on a mouthful of oatmeal. Grandmother gave me a gentle, reproving look, which meant *Don't gobble or guzzle.* I was layered in underwoolens for extra warmth; the dollar for ferry and train fare pressed against my ankle like a hot iron stuck down my boot. The lunch packed in my pretty rose box would last me three days if I rationed it. I was set.

When I went out the door, I slipped the envelope with FINAL NOTICE stamped on it through the letter slot, being careful not to let it clank. I looked back at the house, heart bursting when I thought about what I was doing, how I might never see Grandmother and Rose again.

I glanced up at Ivy's window. I was real glad not to see her smiling down and waving from her safe tower. Even though I was doing the best thing for Grandmother, I was weak all over from sneaking off this way and could barely lift my knees. But I did. I hurried along the walk. I needed to get away as fast as possible. But as soon as I was out of sight, I slowed my steps. I didn't want to take a chance on meeting Aggie or any of the others from school. I didn't know exactly where any of them lived. I hadn't asked, because I didn't want to invite more questions about myself, but now I needed to avoid them. I walked straight south for a ways and then turned east toward the river.

I walked swiftly along past churches and banks, grocers and coopers, confectioners, shoemakers, undertakers, and tobacconists, staying close to businesses. The busy morning sounds of clopping horses, whining trolley wheels, shearing sleigh runners, traffic, and voices filled the main avenue. When I spied a constable, I turned quickly and walked north for a block, then west, away from my school. When I felt safe I headed south again, nearly running, head down, turning and turning again past hotels and saloons, livery stables and black-smiths, until I ran out of sidewalk. I'd reached the ferry landing.

It was colder down here. I shivered, breathed into my cupped hands to warm my face. The sun was still hidden behind the opposite hill across the Hudson. Hard frost glittered coldly on soot-stained snow. My breath puffed out in clouds of white.

I looked out toward the Hudson. I stood there a long time, my heart filled with longing for home and Pa . . . Pa who was strong and good. I wanted to go home to forget all about Grandmother's money troubles and my lies. But Pa would guess; he'd know I'd done something shameful. I didn't want Pa to get a whiff of me, the girl who had forgotten her promise to him that she would always be a Hill Hawk, always be strong and good, hon-est and true. Not affected with put-upon airs, not lying like I'd done with Aggie and Effie, or worse — betraying someone dear, the way I had Grandmother.

Poor, dear Grandmother. What would she do when I didn't come home? She would think of nothing else but me. She would blame herself, and her heart would be broken. I'd made myself believe that running away would help her, but it wouldn't. I was acting like a coward, taking the easy way out . . . for me.

I watched the gray, choppy water, the people gathering their things and beginning to embark on the ferry. Reaching for the dollar in my boot, I started toward the line. It would be easy enough to cross the river and catch the next train, but the sick thought of cowardice spread through me. *I'm not a coward. I'm a Hill Hawk, fierce and strong even in a gale wind.*

I took a deep breath and curled my fingers into fists. I couldn't run away. I couldn't do that to Grandmother. What I needed now was the sort of gumption I'd learned from Pa. I needed to tell Grandmother the truth. No matter what. And maybe I could help. Maybe there was something I could do.

I stood on the wharf for a long time, watching as the ferry moved away and crossed over the river. I let out a slow, ragged breath. Then, gathering my gumption, I started the climb back up the long, steep hill. By the time I got to Grandmother's, the sun was high in the sky, but it was still early to be out of school. Avoiding my reflection in the mirror, I went in quietly, noticing right off that the envelope had been picked up. I hung my cloak on the hall tree and started through the house, heading to the library.

When I set foot in the library, the tray from morning tea was still on the low table, along with the white envelope stamped with the telltale red of the FINAL NOTICE warning. Grandmother and Rose looked alarmed to see me. "Hattie, dear heart, is something wrong?" Grandmother said. Looking flustered, she hurriedly scooped up the evidence, went to her desk, put the letter in a drawer, and locked it up tight. "Why aren't you at school? Nothing is wrong, is it? You look flushed. Oh, dear, you aren't ill?" she said, hurrying back to the chaise.

I shook my head and went to sit beside her. "You don't have to hide that," I said. "I know about the tax notice." I swallowed. "It came yesterday. I hid it because I didn't want to spoil the valentines."

"Hattie, dear, it was wrong of you to do that," Grandmother said, patting my hand. "But it was only one day."

"No," I said. "There was another letter before I started common school." I stopped. Wet my lips. "You were so sad about Grandfather, and the letter said . . . 'payment overdue.' I didn't want to give you more bad news. I thought it could wait."

"It couldn't," Rose muttered.

"Now, Rose," Grandmother said soothingly. "It can wait. It's waited before." She picked up pieces of Grandfather's coat and began to baste the seams and darts that were pinned.

"If you say so," Rose blustered, her eyes snapping. She got to her feet now and picked up the tray.

"But Grandmother . . . could you . . . ? You could . . . Is there anything you could sell?" I asked lamely.

"Hattie, dear, that won't be necessary. It was necessary to give William a burial befitting our station. But taxes?" Grandmother laughed. "Put your mind at ease. You'll see how it is. I'm a Holmes. My father was very prominent," she said in her most aristocratic tone. "That, I assure you, will not be forgotten. Exceptions will be made. Exceptions are always made up here."

I stared at her, unsure. She truly believed that FINAL NOTICE stamped boldly on her tax bill meant nothing. Maybe there wasn't anything to worry about after all.

Giving me a dark look, Rose said, "You can do the washing up, since you're home so early."

"You don't mind, do you, Hattie, dear?" Grandmother said. "Rose and I have nearly finished the suit, but I'd like to keep working. I will wear it when I take this matter up with the authorities."

At the moment, I didn't favor being alone with Rose, but there was no avoiding it. As far as Grandmother was concerned, the tax notice was simply an oversight.

In the kitchen, Rose plunked down the tray on the work table. "A fine pickle you've got us in," she growled. She gave me a long, studied look. "Those taxes can't wait." She flapped her arms; her hands flew in the air. "I thought they'd been paid. I should have guessed. . . ." she muttered thoughtfully.

"No exceptions, you mean? Not even here on the hill?" I asked with a gulp.

"Doubtful," she said, tucking her lips out of sight. "No matter what your grandmother thinks, we've got to do something." Which meant I had to do something.

"Isn't there anything she can sell?" I asked.

Rose just shook her head. Her gloomy air had lost its peppery fire. She looked really grim now. "All I know is taxes on a mansion up here are more than a few trinkets. And after the funeral expense and the headstone . . . But that's none of my affair, not my place to say."

"But if the taxes aren't paid, then what? What will they do?"

Rose shrugged. "She won't tell me what's in the letter. Whatever it is, she's not believing it. Above the law. Hmpf . . . Doubtful, I'd say."

"Oh," I said. A deep chill passed through me like a spirit. I shivered. There really was no money then, nothing. A few heirlooms, trinkets, Rose called them. One thing I did know for sure: whatever the letter said had to be really bad if Grandmother wouldn't even share it with Rose.

Chapter Sixteen

At breakfast the next morning, Grandmother handed me a gray envelope embossed with her monogram. "Take this note to Miss Finster. You will be taking those Regents exams, Hattie, dear," she said proudly.

I might take the exams, but I knew now there was no prospect of attending the Academy. It wasn't even a possibility. Along with the note for Miss Finster, I carried my worries about Grandmother's taxes. Even if the tax collector gave Grandmother grace, she couldn't keep selling her heirlooms, or there would be nothing left but an empty house. It was pretty empty now. And an empty house meant . . . I shivered, not wanting to think about that.

I'd been so worried about the taxes that I forgot to pay attention to other things. Curious how your body can feel things, like when you touch someone and you get a jolt for no reason or you rub against something and your hair crackles and flies all over. Horace said that it was electricity. That's the way my body felt as soon as I walked into the classroom. I felt the crackling, but my seeing, thinking self didn't. I had to be shown. It happened soon enough at recess.

"So," Aggie said, when we were out in the school yard, "how are the plans coming for your party?"

I sighed heavily. There could be no more fairy-tale lies, no more straw spun into gold. "No party," I said. "I . . . we . . ."

"We," Aggie said, cutting me off, "have a new club. We . . . all of us are members. Right, girls?"

Everyone nodded, even Effie.

"Want to know what we call ourselves?" Aggie asked.

I had a nasty feeling that I didn't want to know, but I said, "Okay."

"We are the Brown Dress Society. You can only join if you have a brown dress," Aggie said.

"I don't have one," I said. "You know I don't."

Aggie grinned. Smug. She licked the corners of her mouth. "That's right," she said, sounding surprised that I would admit it.

"Ask your grandmother," Effie said. "She'll have the seamstress make one for you. She will."

I shook my head. "No, she won't."

"She probably thinks brown isn't good enough for your society," Aggie said.

"Probably," I said.

"But if you asked . . ." Effie pleaded with her soft eyes.

"She can't," I said, feeling the heaviness of my lies squashing me down.

"Why can't she?" Aggie asked. "Why not, Hattie?"

The other girls drew closer, watching my face. I knew they expected me to say something smart and important, but I didn't. I stood with my arms hanging down like useless sticks, my heart thudding in fear. Did Aggie know? Had she heard gossip about Grandmother's debt?

"Well, maybe you don't need a brown dress," Aggie said. "I know. We'll let you join if you show us your diamond buckles." She smiled a little meanly.

"I don't have diamond buckles," I said, my tongue feeling as thick as a lump of oatmeal.

"She doesn't have diamond buckles?" Aggie said in a shocked voice. "My, my, I wonder what else she's lied about. Oh, do tell, Hattie."

Her taunts made me want to keep my lies a secret more than ever. But I didn't want to be a liar anymore. No matter what. I took a deep breath and just said it right out. "I lied about a lot of things," I said. "There are no maids. No seamstress. No jewels. No parties with costumes and conundrums. Grandmother has a big house but she has no money. None at all. Not anymore."

Aggie looked smug. "I knew it," she said. "I knew if you were really a rich girl, you wouldn't be going to school with us. I knew you made it up."

"But you live up there, Hattie," Effie said.

"Yes, I do live up there, but that's not where I'm from," I said. I took another deep breath. It wasn't easy to tell, but I owed it to Pa. "I used to live in a cabin over the mountains with my pa," I said. "My pa is a woodsman, a lumberjack, and a raftsman on the river. My ma . . . she . . . she died, and I came to live here with her mother, my grandmother Greymoor." I felt the familiar wrench when I said that Ma was dead. My heart felt like all the blood was being squeezed out until it shattered. "And that's all I have to say about that."

I was shaking real hard, but I felt better inside, like all the pieces of my heart were coming back together the right way. Like I was starting to find the girl who was lost, the real me. Tough and strong. Fearless.

"See, Effie?" Aggie said. "I told you she was just a show-off."

"Aggie's right; I was." My head was throbbing something fierce now. I wet my lips and went on. "I'm sorry, really sorry, that I lied." When you say you are sorry and you really mean it, you think it will make everything better, give you a fresh start. Once, I had been mean to Jasper, my friend back home, but he had kept right on being my friend no fuss or bother. I hoped that would happen now. But it did not.

"You lied," Aggie said. "No taking it back. Sorry doesn't count."

The circle of girls started to break up, but instead of moving away, Effie came up close to me. Soft, sweet Effie. "I know you didn't lie about everything, Hattie," she said quietly. "And I really loved it when you told us about how the chandelier cried rainbows. The way you said it, I could really see it. I could see how the sun would make rainbows splash on the walls like tears . . . even if it was made up." Effie stopped and took a deep breath.

"But you shouldn't have lied about your pa, Hattie. You shouldn't have, but . . ."

Aggie grabbed one of Effie's arms and knotted it through hers. "No buts, Effie," she said in warning. "Hattie doesn't have a brown dress. Remember, we all agreed. Even you," she said meanly.

"It's okay, Effie," I said. And suddenly it was true. It was okay. Strange, but I really didn't care anymore. Not about what Aggie said or did. I was just relieved to have it out with her and over with. In her heart, Effie liked me. It just wasn't in her not to. But Aggie ruled and Effie followed.

Still, I couldn't worry about any of that now. Or brown dresses. Or me. I couldn't worry about me at all. Not now. Now I needed to worry about Grandmother. I would be all right; I could always go home to Pa. But what would happen to Grandmother and Rose?

I started toward the school, but then stopped. I whirled around and walked straight past Aggie and Effie, straight out the gates and into the street.

Chapter Seventeen

I was going to find Horace. Horace would know what to do. Horace always had ideas, and he knew practically everything. He would help me. It's what he would want to do. I felt better just thinking about that.

The Academy wasn't far away, and I might catch him outside for recess. Did the Academy scholars even have recess? I didn't know.

Already from a distance, I could see Horace's head sticking up above a group of boys huddled around him. As I got closer, I could hear his voice and the laughter of the boys.

I stopped at the edge of the school yard, considering. The boys looked really big to me, like grown-ups nearly. I leaned against a tree, half hiding my skinny self behind it. My eyes filmed over, and I felt the pang of sharing someone I didn't want to. Worse, the pain of being left out and forgotten. Horace was happy. His face shone with it. He was king here. This is where he belonged. And I couldn't go over to him. I shouldn't have come.

I started away, but then Horace was there, striding alongside, taking me by the elbow to stop me. "What is it, old dear?" he said with his usual affection. "Nothing wrong?" He looked concerned.

I shook my head. "I wanted to thank you for the valentines. The old ones, me too, we were most surprised and pleased."

"You are most welcome," he said warmly.

"Well . . ." I shifted from foot to foot and then blurted out, "I'm to take the Regents exams for the Academy. Miss Finster recommended me. It's all thanks to you, Horace."

"Jolly good, Hattie. You'll be superb over here. Fit right in. You'll see."

"Thanks." I laughed a little nervously, thinking how I'd probably never get to find out. "I'd better get back. I don't want to keep you, Horace," I said.

"Nothing else on your mind?" he said, tilting his head to study my face.

"No . . . no, that was it," I said.

"Jolly good then," he said, smiling. "Tell the old ones I'll stop in with a treat for all of us as soon as I get a day free."

I nodded and watched as he sprinted away. When he got a free day, he would come. But that might not be soon enough. He would see how things were for himself. But any money he had would already have been spent on feasty foods, books, and artful things. Horace had the best heart, but he wasn't the saving-for-a-rainy-day sort.

It all seemed hopeless as I started for home. I had made a mess of everything. I had made up a fairy tale to make friends. I'd betrayed Grandmother. I'd believed I could fix everything with a hidden fortune that didn't exist. I had waited too long to tell Grandmother about the letter. I'd done everything wrong. And I could see no fix to it.

There had to be something I could do. I just needed to . . . to . . . I needed a plan. A good plan. And I needed it fast.

But good plans for making money fast are not that easy to come up with when you are eleven, almost twelve, and don't know how to do or make anything.

I couldn't sew in a straight line. Couldn't cook without burning the food. There must be something I could do. But what?

And then it hit me. Grandmother had a big house with lots and lots of empty rooms. We could open a boarding house for schoolteachers.

That night I couldn't sleep. All I could think about was making a good plan and putting it into action. We already had some experience with boarders because of Horace. We'd all waited on Horace when he was with us, though he had helped us out, too. In a way, I was like a boarder, even though I had regular chores to do every day and helped with the cleaning, the wash, and the ironing. I would give up my room and sleep downstairs in the little room next to Rose's. I could do the running upstairs and downstairs, bringing fresh water and changing the linens, sweeping and dusting. I could set the table, clear, and do dishes. We could all eat together.

And the boarders would have to do some things for themselves. I was pretty sure that was the way it worked. No men allowed, unless Horace came back. I had no idea about what to charge, but it would have to be paid in advance. Three meals a day, tea, and a lovely room should be enough to pay the taxes.

I grabbed my tablet and set it all down neatly like an ad in the *Daily Freeman*. ROOMS TO LET IN KINGSTON. FASHIONABLE NEIGHBORHOOD. MEALS PROVIDED. RATES REASONABLE. PAYMENT IN ADVANCE. REFERENCES REQUIRED. WOMEN ONLY. SCHOOLTEACHERS PREFERRED. (I figured that women usually were more willing to join in or take care of their ownselves than men, who eschewed such things as housework, Horace being the exception.) INQUIRE AT RESIDENCE OF MRS. W. H. GREYMOOR. And then we could write the address. Grandmother could put my ad in the paper. That should work.

In the morning, Grandmother still didn't mention the taxes. Pink colored her cheeks, and her voice had its songbird twitter again. The suit would be done in no time at all, she said.

Rose simply grunted and muttered something. Her eyes were puffy slits and darkly circled, her face dented by frown lines.

I took a deep breath. Grandmother would have to listen. "Grandmother," I said, "I have a plan, a way to pay the taxes."

Grandmother blinked. "Hattie, dear heart, don't

worry yourself about it. I'm sure they will give us grace . . . under the circumstances of William's recent demise."

"Hortensia," Rose said gently, "hear the girl out."

I reached down and grabbed my tablet from the floor. "Look, I've planned it all out in lists. These are the rooms we can use. These are the chores each of us will have to do. This is the list of things the others will have to do."

"Others. What others? Whatever do you mean?" Grandmother asked.

I hadn't wanted to blurt out the idea of a boarding house, since I was pretty sure Grandmother wouldn't approve right off. But I had to now. "A boarding house for schoolteachers," I said. "Here's the ad I wrote for the paper, and we . . . I can ask Miss Finster if she knows of anyone."

"You most certainly will not. The shame of it, of having the whole town know . . . Mrs. Greymoor the third taking in boarders, indeed not."

"I'll clean the rooms, fetch the water, take care of the dining room," I said.

"Absolutely not," Grandmother said. "I am not waiting on schoolteachers, and you will be going to the Academy."

Rose shook her head. "Think of all the extra food to buy. All the extra cooking. Why I'd never get off my feet."

"Extra coal, extra gas, extra kerosene," Grandmother said. "Such expense, dear child . . . We might as well pay the boarders to stay here."

"I'll be the maid, the serving girl, the kitchen help," I said. "We'll charge them in advance." I was beginning to feel desperate. "We have to do something or we'll end up . . ." I caught the look on both their faces, as if I had personally ushered Misfortune into the room. I stopped that *poorhouse* word from coming out of my mouth.

"You've forgotten our station, Hattie. Your station," Grandmother said quietly. And that was the end of that. For her. But not for me.

Chapter Eighteen

Things seemed even more hopeless now. A boarding house really had seemed like the best plan, better than . . . than what? What else could I do?

Something, probably, but nothing Grandmother would approve of. Maybe I could find a job. I would have to skip school to do that, but I couldn't think of any other way to find work. First I'd look for Help Wanted signs in store windows. I was good at ciphering, and Grandmother had taught me how to be polite and proper. I could sweep floors, put out new merchandise, wait on customers. Maybe it would be as easy as that.

But it was not easy. There were no Help Wanted signs in the stores closest to Grandmother's. I decided to ask in one anyway—Wadsworth Stationery and Books, where I had gotten my lace hearts.

I went up to the saleswoman behind the counter. She had puffy white curls and too much face powder. It made her look sort of like a melting snowman. I suspected she was the owner's wife. "Pardon me, madame, may I inquire, please, if you need a good girl for helping out? I can cipher, and sweep, stock shelves, run errands, write ads for the paper. My penmanship is quite good. I can speak French, a little German, read Latin." I was surprised at how much I really did know.

"You sound highly qualified for such a young lady," she said. I saw her suspicious, considering look. "You don't look like a girl in need of employment." She cleared her throat. "And it's a boy we would need for more strenuous labor—lifting, feeding the coal to the stove, deliveries—when business picks up."

"But I can do those things. I'm strong. I'm not afraid of heavy labor."

She shook her head. "I'm afraid not, dear. A domestic placing would be more suitable. One of the families on the hill would surely hire you," she said.

I pressed my lips together and looked down. "Please, ma'am," I whispered, swallowing hard to keep back tears.

She cleared her throat. "But . . . of course, my eyesight isn't what it used to be. Perhaps," she said, her tone softer now, "in the spring. Part-time. Ledger entries, accounts. Small wage to start."

I nodded. "Thank you, madame, for your kindness," I said with a slight curtsy.

"Stop back in April then," she said with a nod.

Things were not going well. I stepped outside. The wind had picked up. Cinders and litter swirled along the avenue. Pages of discarded newspaper flapped like birds' wings. I snatched a page that had wrapped itself around a lamppost. It was nearly shredded. The date was January. But a newspaper was what I needed. It would have Help Wanted ads. Lots of possibilities. I folded it up small and took it along.

I knew papers were often left on the trolley, but I'd need a ticket or a dime for a ride. I had neither. I could still go to the trolley station. I could watch for gentlemen carrying papers folded under an arm. If the paper wasn't neat and tight, it'd been read. I spotted one in no time at all.

"May I have your paper, sir?" I asked.

The man drew back and scowled, then bustled away like a fat bumblebee. There must be a better way. Easier, like grabbing a paper and running with it. But what if I got caught? I sighed. I'd try again when the next trolley came, study the faces first as the men disembarked. The first one had heavy jowls and a scowl, probably mean. Then came a man with a weak chin and scared rabbity eyes. Next was a thin, studious sort with a preoccupied look. Worth a try. "Please, sir, are you through with your paper?"

"How did you know?" he asked in surprise.

"The pages . . . they're ruffled, sir."

"Why, yes, they are. Quite the little observer," he said, handing it to me. "Meant to leave it on the trolley. Absentminded, you see."

"Thank you, sir," I said.

"Better hurry to catch up with your governess," he said, nodding to a young woman with a young child in tow.

"Yes, I'll do that, sir," I said with a little curtsy. "Good day, then." But fortunately I was already forgotten, and he was headed off to his destination.

Chapter Nineteen

I hurried up the sidewalk toward Grandmother's and was surprised to see Ivy come running down her drive. "Wait," she called softly.

I stopped as she ran up, breathless, and nearly flung herself against the iron fence. "What have you been doing every day? Aren't you going to school?"

"Mostly," I said cautiously. "Should you be talking to me?"

Ivy bit her lip. "No," she said quietly. "But I don't care." She looked up into my eyes, and I caught my breath. She was my friend. I saw true sincerity in her eyes. Not like Aggie, who had always studied me in a watchful, calculating way, like a cat waiting to pounce on its prey.

"All right," I said. "I'll tell you what I've been doing." After all, what did I have to lose? "Grandmother doesn't know, Ivy, so you have to promise to keep it a secret. Promise? Cross your heart?"

"Promise," Ivy said, crossing her heart. She was wearing an emerald coat with brown fur today. Horace would have cooed over it. Effie, too.

"It's like this," I said. "Yesterday I decided to run away and go home to my pa. Today I skipped school to look for work." It sounded pretty outrageous. More wild than my lies. "Grandmother is in trouble. Big tax troubles, but she acts like it's nothing. I've got to save her," I said. "You wouldn't need a serving girl or an upstairs maid, a lady's maid or anything? Or know of anyone who might?"

Ivy shook her head. "I know about your troubles. Mother said . . ." Ivy broke off. She bit her lip and looked down. "She dotes on gossip," she said, looking up at me now. Ivy looked distressed and a little embarrassed. "It wouldn't do for you to work for one of us."

"But I could, right? Why not?"

"It would be too horrible." Ivy pressed her lips together as if she didn't want to say it. But she did. "It'd be scullery work, Hattie. Bottom of the heap, a pittance, or nothing but lodging and meals."

"If there is any work for wages, anything at all, I'll do it. I can do it. I've worked in the woods with Pa, chopped firewood, cooked, milked a cow, dressed like a boy, rafted logs on the river . . . but Grandmother hasn't. She only knows how to be a lady."

Ivy's mouth went round in awe, but she shook her head. "Don't do it. You shouldn't, Hattie, please," Ivy said. "Don't work unless you absolutely must. Then I'd ask for something else, something better, not a maid." I could see by her face that she had no idea what sort of work that would be. She reached through the bars of the black iron fence and squeezed my hand. She smelled like spring and lilies of the valley.

Ivy glanced over her shoulder, then back at me. "If you need me, come round to the back door. The house-keeper won't mind. She won't tell."

"Okay," I whispered. Hot tears pricked my eyes. I blinked them away. Ivy wanted to help, but what could she possibly do that I couldn't do for myself? I took a shaky breath and headed into the house.

Grandmother was busy hand-stitching her suit, and Rose was in the kitchen. Something smelled like sweet and spicy fruit, a compote maybe, which meant that Rose was missing Horace. I hurried up to my room, spread the newspaper out on my bed, and began my search.

First I looked at the Help Wanted ads. Salesman. Painter. Housekeeper. Cook. Chambermaid. Governess. I circled *chambermaid.* I wasn't exactly sure what one of those did, but I thought they cleaned the upstairs bedrooms, *chambers* to rich folk. I could ask Grandmother what it meant, but that would make her suspicious. I sighed and turned the page. *Rooms to let. Store to let. For sale— two wood-frame houses. For sale—large three-story house.*

I turned the page. Railroad schedule for times and destinations. Times and ticket charges for the trolley and ferry. Post office schedules for Rondout and Kingston.

I turned the page and studied the ads.

⧆ *TUTT'S PILLS FOR TORPID BOWELS* ⧆

EXCAVATING APPARATUS FOR CESSPOOLS

HORSES! HORSES! HORSES!
FOR SALE

HUMPHREY'S HOMEOPATHIC CURE
for all diseases of horses, cows, pigs

Down at the very bottom in the left-hand corner, I saw, *Art, needlework, and painting. Classes forming at my rooms.* I circled that one. It gave me an idea of something we could add to the boarding house for elegance and enhancement. Nothing else struck me.

I took the tattered page from the January paper and smoothed it out. My hand stopped dead, and a chill went through me when my eye fell on the word TAXES. There was a big notice in large print: CITY TAXES — TREASURER'S NOTICE. Quickly, I scanned through the lines and went from cold to solid ice when I read:

days after written notice, I shall proceed without delay to have delinquent taxes collected by distress and sale of goods at public auction as required by the city charter.

Days? How many days? That piece was torn. And whose goods were to be sold? There were no names listed. But it could mean Grandmother. She'd already gotten more than one written notice of unpaid taxes.

Feeling very sick, I knew that things were a lot worse than I'd thought. If only I had given Grandmother the first notice. If only I had known what was in it. I had wasted all that time solving Grandfather's code and then searching for any other way but the right one. The notice said "days." How many days? Not many, I was sure.

Chapter Twenty

I still hadn't decided whether to go to school when I started out the next morning, but when I reached the corner, I kept on going. I would talk to Miss Finster. A boarding house was still our best chance, especially with rents to be paid in advance.

My lunch box was still in the cloakroom on the floor beneath my hook, but someone had eaten my lunch. I walked down the aisle, walked between Aggie on one side and Effie on the other. Aggie was staring at Effie, giving her a warning look. Effie bent her head as I passed by. No one spoke as I took my seat up front by Miss Finster and bent over my algebra book to start work on story problems.

I loved algebra. I was good at it. I loved the trysting trains starting in different directions, the pipes and rate of flow and quarts it took to fill a cistern, the time it took Tom and John to paint a lamppost if they started at different times and worked at different speeds. I loved $x + y = z$. I could solve these problems every time. It made me feel as if I could find a solution to Grandmother's problems, too. Algebra made my insides calm down and my jitters stop. It made my head stop spinning like a toy top.

After school, I didn't have to approach Miss Finster, because she asked me to stay. I was ready to blurt out my plans for a boarding house, but she raised a hand to shush me. "Miss Finster is glad to see you buckling down to work today. But she is very disturbed about your truancy and the way you've slacked off on your studies. She is troubled by your sudden change in behavior."

The teacher stopped and pressed her fingers against her temples, squinting as if she might have a headache. "It is an honor to be selected for the Academy. And Miss Finster is proud of us . . . of you. Only the best students with the best school records and attendance are accepted.

You will not let us down, will you, Hattie? If . . . if there is something else, something wrong . . ."

"I'm sorry, Miss Finster. I promise to do better."

"Miss Finster is glad to hear it. Now, was there something you wanted to ask?"

"Yes," I said, blurting out my plan. "We're opening a boarding house for schoolteachers. Women only," I added quickly, seeing the look of shock on her face. "The rooms are lovely. It's in a fashionable neighborhood. We have a wonderful cook. If you don't need a room, would you know of anyone who might?"

The teacher looked down. She stared out the window. Then she looked at me. "Dear child, we had no idea. Miss Finster is most sorry for your trouble. We'll see what we can do."

"Thank you," I said. When I got outside, it had started to snow. Aggie simply stared at me, her face like a stone. Effie looked away, pretending she didn't see me. I had wanted to speak to her. But now I knew it was better not to. I might never be coming back here, and it wouldn't be fair to single her out and upset things.

By now, the snow was coming down hard. So I hurried away, hurried to get home and talk to Grandmother again about the boarding house. Already, as I started up the hill to Grandmother's, the sidewalks were wet and slippery, and the heavy snow was sticking to everything.

When I was almost to the house, a horse-drawn wagon clip-clopped past me. The horse was black. The wagon was black, with bright gold letters painted on the outside. Through the heavy curtain of falling snow, I saw CITY OF KINGSTON arcing across the side, with SHERIFF beneath it. The wagon halted in front of Grandmother's. My heart leaped like a trout in my chest and then promptly flopped on its side, dead cold.

A man in black jumped down from the high seat and tied the reins to the stone hitching post. Another man was climbing down now. He was meaty, like a beefy bull. Thick arms, thick neck, chest like a barrel. He wore a long black coat with a brassy bright star on it.

"Please, sir," I said, running up. "May I help you?"

The big man scowled, then swung away from me and started to the gate.

"You shouldn't go in there," I said.

"And why not?" he said, frowning.

"They're sick," I said. "They should be quarantined." I was especially serious about that.

"Quarantined?" The younger man, who had tied up the horses, looked a mite spooked.

"Quarantined? There's no sign saying it on the door."
The older man shook the snow from his tall hat and kept
on walking.

"I wouldn't go in there," I said. "They're contagious.
You'll get sick. Maybe die."

"We will, will we?" The older man stopped and turned
around. "And just what is this dread sickness, little miss?"

What was it? What should I say? Cholera? No.
Consumption? No. Our house would be already posted
for those. There was a word lolling around on my tongue.
I didn't know what it meant, but it sounded pretty serious. "Lumbago," I said, recalling the word I'd seen in the
newspaper ad.

The two men looked shocked. They looked at each
other. And then they burst out laughing. Not a little laugh,
but a huge belly-aching laugh that made their stomachs
jiggle like pudding.

I shook my head. Bad choice.

"Nice try, kid," the sheriff said.

"Oh, my lumbago. It hurts so much," the deputy
quipped.

"We'll have to quarantine you for that one, son." The
two men went on up the walk, guffawing and slapping
their legs merrily.

127

I trailed behind. Laughing was a good sign. They were feeling jolly now, in a good mood. As soon as they got to the porch, I raced ahead and beat them to the door. I spread myself across it, hanging tight to the knob. "My grandmother is really old. My grandfather just died, and she's really sad and we have no food."

The sheriff simply tore my hand off the knob and pushed against the door. He didn't look so jolly anymore. I thought it was probably a good idea if I didn't kick him or bite his hand. He looked like he might arrest me and throw me in his wagon.

"Open the door," he ordered now, his bushy eyebrows meeting in the middle.

So I gulped and did as he said.

"Hattie, dear, is that you?" Grandmother said in a lilting bird voice. She was standing just inside in front of the mirror, admiring herself in her altered walking suit and trimmed bonnet. "What do you think?" she said. Turning around, she saw the men. I thought she would swoon for sure, but I should have known Grandmother better than that. When you've always lived a privileged life, you never consider that the underprivileged would have the temerity to darken your door. It just didn't happen up here.

"Why, gentlemen," she greeted them airily, "I was about to pay you a visit. So delighted that you've saved me the inconvenience. Is that snow?" she asked, peering past them to the street.

The two men gave each other an amused look.

I lowered my head. We were doomed for sure.

"You're looking well today, Mrs. Greymoor," the sheriff said, raising a scornful eyebrow at me.

"That's *Holmes* Greymoor the third," she corrected. "Please, won't you come into the drawing room?"

"Ma'am, this is not a social call. Nothing of the sort. You are hereby notified, my deputy as witness, that you are officially served with a Warrant of Seizure and Distraint. You may not leave town. You may not sell anything on or in these premises. We are authorized by the tax collector, City of Kingston, to list the contents of your household—that means all movable goods, articles of clothing being the exception."

"Don't you know who I am?" Grandmother asked, still unruffled.

"Yes," the sheriff said. "I know you don't pay your taxes." He slapped the warrant, which had a bright gold seal on it, into her hands and turned to his deputy. "Might as well start here. Write this down for the auction."

"Auction?" Grandmother said, her smile fading. "What auction?"

He shook his head. "One crystal chandelier, hall tree, hall table, gilded mirror."

"Wait," I said. "Hold it just a minute. The chandelier is attached. It's not movable," I said hotly.

"Cross that one out," he said, giving me a black look.

"Cross out gilded mirror, too," I said. "It's part of the wall. See for yourself."

He shook his head. "Come on, Humphrey." He brushed us aside and started toward the stairs as though this weren't somebody's home. "Let's start at the top floor."

"Nice woodwork," the deputy said, whistling as he looked around at the hand-carved flowers on the walnut paneling. "You can keep that."

"You men, stop," Grandmother said. "Have you no manners?"

"Nothing to do with manners, ma'am," the sheriff said. "No fault in upholding the law. The sooner we go through the house and write down everything to be sold, the sooner we'll be gone."

I saw the lights go down in Grandmother's eyes as the truth settled in. There was no grace for her. Being from a prominent family made no difference. The law was the law. They were here to take stock and sell her possessions. I wanted to cry as she withered on the spot, slumped down on the hall chair, her fingers automatically working the lace at her throat.

"Is anything up there locked?" the sheriff asked.

"Yes," I hissed.

"Well, what are you waiting for? Get the keys."

Anger pounding through me, I fled down the hall to the library, grabbed Grandmother's ring of house keys from her desk drawer, and ran back. I didn't want to leave Grandmother alone with them any longer than necessary.

The sheriff let me pass to go up the stairs ahead of him. The old servants' quarters were empty, so I opened that door first.

"Gaw," the deputy said. "Nothing here, empty as a—"

"Gunnysack with a hole in it," I finished for him.

"Yeah, that's it," he said, looking surprised to hear such a crude expression coming from a girl on the hill.

The third-story schoolroom was locked, because the door wouldn't stay closed otherwise. It was strange going in without Horace here. The room was just as we left it. Horace's large, looping handwriting gracefully sprawled across the chalkboard; a few of his books, his trunk, and some of his summer clothes were still in his rooms.

"The books and trunk belong to my former tutor," I said. "He'll be coming to collect them when he has a free day."

The deputy poked around. "Nothing of value here," he said. "Junk man's lot."

"Write it down," the sheriff said. "Auction it last. Make a note of that."

I traipsed down the steps to the second floor and opened doors along the corridor. The locked rooms were empty except for dark drapes covering the windows.

"Gaw," the deputy said. "Never expected . . ."

"Hard times on the hill," I said bitingly. I hesitated then, because now we were standing in front of my mother's room. I had to open the door for them, but I didn't want them to see, and I didn't want them touching her things. Her room was just the way she had left it thirteen years before, when she'd run away with my Pa and married him. I trembled as I slowly pushed open the door.

"Why, this is more like it," the sheriff said. "There's good stuff here."

"Look at the dust and cobwebs. Spooky," the deputy said. "Creepy, like a tomb."

"It's my mother's room," I said softly. "She died."

For a second, both men were still. Then the sheriff coughed. "Marble angels, canopy bed, violet lamp . . ." he said. "Write it down."

Every breath hurt. It was my fault. It was more than furniture in here; it was pieces of my mother. And now it would be auctioned. What had I done? I swallowed and swallowed, but the sobs kept wanting to come.

A heavy hand patted my shoulder. "It's our job, missy," the sheriff said. "We don't got no choice about what stays and what goes. It's all gotta be writ down." He scuffled his feet. "Let's move along, now."

I took a deep breath and nodded. There was just my room and Grandmother's left up here. Everything was done sober-like. It was the downstairs that had all the best heirlooms—dining room, drawing room, kitchen, library. We moved swiftly along, all of us just wanting it over with.

Grandmother and Rose were in the library, having tea and cakes as if it were a normal day. They sipped their tea, Grandmother sitting stiff as a bristle with her aura of frost to protect her, while the men moved around them, writing things down—lamps, chaise, wing chairs, books, desk, clocks, rugs, tables . . . but they couldn't write down the memories, the good years, the hard times, the cozy, sweet afternoon teas with Horace and how the room always glowed when we were all together.

It seemed that things could not get any worse that day. I was wrong. I followed the sheriff and deputy to the door, the deputy going ahead out to the wagon.

"Sheriff, sir," I said. "Is there any way to stop this?"

"It's all in the warrant, but so as you know, it's not just taxes now. There's fines and fees, interest, wages, public notice of sale in the papers at the courthouse . . ." He ticked them off on his thick fingers.

"How can Grandmother pay her taxes if she can't sell anything?"

The sheriff shrugged. "That's not my concern."

The deputy was back. This time he had a hammer and signs. "Where do you want these?"

"Nail one up here by the door. Put another on the gate," the sheriff said.

I wanted to cover my ears when the deputy struck blows, driving nails into the painted white siding, the sound reporting like a rifle shot even with the softening cover of the falling snow. I wanted to rip the notice off the house. I wanted to beat my fists against the sheriff. I wanted to blame him. But I couldn't; it wasn't his fault.

Once they were gone, I read the sign:

> NOTICE OF SALE AT PUBLIC AUCTION OF PERSONAL PROPERTY FOR UNPAID TAXES. NOTICE HEREBY GIVEN:
> That the described personal property posted at Ulster County Courthouse will be sold at public auction at premises of said Mrs. W. E. Holmes Greymoor III, in the City of Kingston on the twenty-seventh day of February, at the hour of 2 p.m. of said day.

I leaned against the house to cover up the sign and catch my breath. There was nothing I could do to stop the sale. Even if I worked for Ivy's family, I'd never make enough money to pay for anything. Not even close. I clenched my fists and squeezed back the tears. It was time to go in and face Grandmother.

Chapter Twenty-one

When I opened the door, there was the gilt-framed mirror that still hid the first tax letter that could have prevented public disgrace. But now nothing here was Grandmother's to sell. Everything here was under house arrest by a Warrant of Seizure and Distraint.

If only . . . if only I could go back and fix things, go back and do the day over, give Grandmother the tax notice, but whoever got to do that? Nobody. A dull ache moved through me and settled in my heart. I turned away from the face of the girl in the mirror and went down the hall to the library.

When I walked into the room, Grandmother patted the empty spot on the chaise beside her. Rose poured me some tea.

"It's all very simple, really." Grandmother's frosty stare had melted from her face. She looked ashen now and very tired. "I have failed," she said in a calm, matter-of-fact way. "All of our possessions will be auctioned in a handful of days. What was I thinking? The funeral, the burial, the headstone . . . didn't need to be . . . but how could I do less for poor William? I have failed my father, who gave me everything. I have failed you, Rose, my dearest friend. I have failed you, Hattie." Grandmother got up and went to her desk. "There is nothing to be done but write your father to come and get you. How harshly I judged him, but it is I who have failed as your guardian. I cannot meet your needs." She took a sheet of gray stationery, picked up her pen, and dipped the nib in ink.

I swallowed. Grandmother was making it too easy for me. It would be easy to let her write the letter, easy to let her take the blame. But I was the one who needed to write the letter, to tell Pa the truth about me. I couldn't let Grandmother take the blame for what I'd done.

"Please don't write Pa. Not now," I said. "We're not giving up, Grandmother. I'm staying to help."

"Hattie, dear," Grandmother said, a little color returning to her cheeks. "Very well." She looked around at all the things that were dear to her. "The warrant says that the auction will end as soon as the taxes and expenses are satisfied. I suppose we will be left with something."

I took a deep breath. "Suppose we make a list of the dearest things — small things. We'll set them aside, out of the way."

"We can do that, Hortensia," Rose said.

"Yes, I see," Grandmother said. I watched them pondering, but nothing was getting written down. Finally, Grandmother dropped her hands in her lap and sighed. "It's no good, Hattie. The idea is sound, but we have the sheriff to consider. If we take matters into our own hands, he will deliberately thwart us. I am most certain about that."

"But we won't move anything out of the house," I said. "They have a list of what's in every room, but some things always get moved from place to place. Things like the sterling silver tea set."

"Yes," Rose said, her eyes brightening. "Things like the crystal cordial glasses."

"It is best," Grandmother said, "to leave things just as

they are and go on these last few days as if nothing will change."

"But what does it hurt to put a few things out of sight? Special things, Grandmother, not everything."

"Hattie's right," Rose said, rising from her chair. "One or two things put . . . put . . ."

"In the pantry," I said quickly. "On the top shelf. In the back."

"Yes, that might work," Grandmother said, a little spark returning to her eyes. "We'll put a few things out of sight, but not hidden, exactly." Grandmother looked thoughtful. "Even if the Academy is impossible now . . ." she said, her voice quavering, "it is imperative that you take the Regents exams. You must."

"Of course, Grandmother," I said. It seemed a silly thing to bother with now, but it would make Grandmother feel better, and I wanted to prove to myself that I could do it. I took a deep breath. There was one more possibility that none of us had mentioned. "There's still Cousin Ernest," I said. Ernest Holmes was Grandmother's first cousin, her only relative besides me. He'd taken charge of running the shipping business for her after Grandfather was put in the asylum. "He would want to help."

Grandmother shook her head. "I am afraid things are worse than you know. I wired Ernest as soon as I received the notice. He responded immediately. I assure you that he would help if he could, but he has struggles of his own, loans and mortgages . . . hanging on till spring, when river travel picks up."

I bowed my head. The ticking of the clocks seemed so loud now, counting time in an unhappy silence when things go wrong and no one speaks.

Finally, Grandmother spoke. "Don't blame yourself, Hattie," she said gently. "It isn't as if I hadn't known the taxes would go to collection. I did count on grace, if not forgiveness."

But no matter what Grandmother said, I deserved a huge parcel of the blame. One thing that I knew for sure: the auction was going to take place. There was nothing we could do. No way to stop it now. I had no idea about what would happen after that.

Chapter Twenty-two

School on Monday was out of the question. There was too much to tend to here. Despite Grandmother's insistence that things were to go on as usual, that nothing was to change, everything had to change. There were drawers to go through, decisions to be made about what to do with the things that weren't to be sold. Did the draperies count? What about the linens, the lace doilies, tablecloths, and antimacassars? What about bedding? What about fabrics and yarns and buttons? If it wasn't on the sheriff's list, did that mean it was ours?

The things we knew we could keep still had to be sorted through. We had to decide where to put our clothes, our letters and cards, our personal things before the day of the sale. Would they dump out the drawers or carry out furniture with our belongings still in cupboards and bureaus, trunks and chests? We didn't know. But we couldn't leave anything to Chance. Everything had to be gone through.

We were in quite a frenzy trying to think of everything. By afternoon, the old ones were worn out and simply toppled into the wing chairs. I made the tea and brought it out with biscuits and jam, rolling the tea cart down the hall to the library, along with the silver tea set, the best china, and teaspoons.

Just as I poured the tea, the grinding noise of the doorbell sounded from the front hall. We looked at each other, alarmed. The same question was written on all our faces. "What now?" Grandmother said.

Rose shook her head. "Beelzebub probably."

"I'll go," I said, hurrying out to answer the door, a queasy feeling in my stomach. Maybe it was Ivy. It could be Horace. It didn't have to be bad news. Cautiously, I opened the door. It was two women who looked oddly familiar.

My face got instantly hot, and I started to sweat. There was no way that the blinding print of the PUBLIC

NOTICE could be missed. Their eyes shifted back and forth from the signs to me.

"We're here about lodging," the younger of the two said. They both wore sturdy brown coats of good wool.

"Miss Finster said you were boarding teachers, women only," the older of the two said. "We were sure this was the right address. . . ."

"But we must have copied it wrong," the younger one said, looking at the scrap of paper in her hand. It was obvious to me that we all knew they were at the right place, and it was my responsibility to say so. I sighed. It was just one more reminder of what I'd done wrong.

"It is the right place," I said. "I'm very sorry for your trouble, but . . ."

"Yes, we see . . . we . . . oh, dear," said the younger.

"We'll just be going, then," said the elder. It was clear that they were as uncomfortable about our troubles as I was.

"Thank you, then." I closed the door and went back to tell the old ones that someone had come calling to the wrong house.

* * *

The next morning, I set out for Kingston Academy. I was a little worried about the exams but not too worried about finding where I should go or getting to the right place. Others from schools in town and out of town would be taking the exams. I'd just join in.

When I drew near the school, there were lots of students milling around, but Horace stood watching for me at the edge of the crowd. He strode down the walk to meet me.

"Hey, old dear," he said. "Are you set?"

"I think so," I said, my heart gladdened by the sight of him.

He bent down a little and lowered his voice. "It'll be a cinch for you, Hattie. Even the mathematics," he said. "Grrr, I should have done more of those silly word problems with you."

I didn't tell him that I'd been working hard on algebra with Miss Finster and on my own. I didn't want him to feel bad about that. "You made every school lesson extraordinary, a scrumptious feast," I said.

"I did, didn't I? It was lovely, wasn't it?" he said almost wistfully.

"And I've brought you some ham and dumplings

along with ugly rutabagas and parsnips," I said, wrinkling my nose as I handed him the box from Rose.

"Jolly excellent," Horace said, taking the box. He peeked in and inhaled with a gusto that made me giggle. Then he became the teacher again. "I'll drop you off at the exam room and come back at the end of the day. I've arranged it so I can walk you home and stay for a visit with the old ones. We'll catch up on all the good gossipy stuff."

"Oh, Horace, that would please them so much," I said, momentarily relieved that I didn't have to blurt out the bad news. It could wait. What I had to do now was concentrate on the exams and do my best.

The time passed swiftly, and Horace collected me at the end of the day. We chattered about the exams, which were not bad, I told him cautiously. "But I didn't know every single answer."

Horace laughed. "You're much too modest," he said. "You forget, my dear, that I know exactly how well you do on exams."

"Mostly," I agreed. "But I don't do well with

everything, Horace." Then, as we walked up the avenue to Grandmother's, I told him about my misdeeds at school, about my fairy-tale lies, and all about Aggie and Effie. Then I told him about the tax notices I hid and Grandfather's code book that did not lead to a fortune, about running away and about looking desperately for a job.

Horace looked thoughtfully troubled. "That's what you came to tell me, wasn't it? About your misdeeds and Grandmother's money concerns?"

"Yes," I said, and went right on in a rush. "But right after that, things got worse. The sheriff came, Horace. He went through the whole house top to bottom, writing everything down that Grandmother owned. His deputy put up public notice signs for an auction. And now the public auction is published in the papers."

"Dreadfully odious," he muttered.

Woefully I added, "The auction is tomorrow at two o'clock."

"Tomorrow?" Horace was aghast. "Hattie, why didn't you tell me? Why did you hide this from me . . . *me*?" he said, horribly wounded now.

"Because I . . . none of us wanted to spoil your good fortune."

"But we're like family."

"We are, Horace," I said.

"And it does help to tell someone our troubles . . . someone to whom it matters."

"It does," I said, and I did feel better. Things didn't seem as huge and horrible as before, even though they were. But the main thing for me was that Horace kept right on being my friend even though he knew the very worst things about me. "Oh, Horace, it is good to get it all out."

"And it will all come right somehow. Things always do," he said as if to convince both of us, though he didn't say how or offer any solutions. No matter. He was here, and that would be a good tonic for the old ones.

We were at Grandmother's gate then, but I didn't see Ivy watching for me at the window. I knew she wanted to be my friend, but maybe she wouldn't have enough courage—like Effie. Could Ivy go against her mother any more than Effie had gone against Aggie? Not likely, not after the whole neighborhood had witnessed the sheriff coming. Not likely, with the public notices in bold black letters nailed to the gate and the house. Not likely, with the notice published in all the newspapers. Never ever after the auction. Grandmother would be the gossipy buzz among all the old society families. And that would be the end of that.

Chapter Twenty-three

For a little while, the darkness of what was to come was pushed away by Horace's visit. Rose immediately went off to concoct a special dinner and bring out a fruity summer cordial to celebrate. So that is how things went the night before the auction.

Grandmother and I lit all the lamps, the candles in the candelabra and candlesticks, all the gaslights in the dining room and the hall. We used the best linen on the table, the best china and silver, the Dorflinger crystal and cut glass. The dining room glowed. It was a magical evening with no darkness in it. No tears. No long faces. Just celebration and Horace reading Shakespeare's *Much Ado About Nothing* to gladden the night.

The next morning, I wished for gloom and darkness, gray clouds and snow, but the sun was bright and reality knocked early. The sheriff and his deputy were at the door before noon, along with several men who looked and smelled like they'd been picked up from the gutter outside a saloon door. The deputy was holding the list. The sheriff went off to the library with Grandmother to go over the sale procedures.

And before long, the first of the carriages was beginning to arrive. The auction and the work of moving things would begin soon. I planted myself next to the sheriff on the porch and watched as the avenue filled up, carriages standing in a long row, stretching in both directions. I looked over at the house next door. No sign of Ivy in her upstairs window. And if her mother were watching, she was discreetly hidden.

The pieces of furniture that I had seen every day and lived with, things I knew were my mother's, my grandmother's, my great-grandmother's and even before that, things that had belonged to my ancestors whom I didn't know at all, were now passed from the deputy's hands to strangers standing in the snowy yard or on the walk or in the street. I searched the crowd to see if there was anyone I knew, but it was all men looking like crows in their somber suits.

Things that had been touched by only us were fingered and touched by others, our memories rubbed out by their hands—the violet lamp, the marble angels, the silverware, crystal, candelabra, china, the Gillow chairs and telescopic table brought from England. Once things were brought outside, they looked diminished and changed. No longer this family's. No longer Grandmother's. No longer from this house. Sold. Sold. Sold.

Finally, the sheriff lowered his gavel. This time he said, "Sale over." Then he turned to me. "Are you okay, young miss?" he asked. I thought he looked at me differently, surprised, I think, that I had stuck it out to the end, standing by him, keeping a close eye on the receipts to make sure Grandmother wasn't cheated.

"What happens now?" I asked.

"Nothing," he said, stuffing the last of the receipts into a banker's bag. "The taxes are paid, the fines and expenses. Your grandmother is free." He started to go, but then turned back. "You're a brave youngster," he said. "You got something strong inside. Tough. I respect that."

Then they were gone. The strangers, the carriages, the sheriff and his men.

I walked out to the gate and ripped PUBLIC NOTICE off the gate, then went back to the house and ripped that one off, too. I ripped them to shreds. We were no longer public. What was left wasn't much, but it was enough. For a while at least, until debt began to mount and taxes came due again. But for now, Grandmother still had her silver tea set, Rose the cherished cordial glasses.

We didn't talk about it, Grandmother, Rose, and I. We all set about making order, cleaning up mud, cigar ash, spittle, slushy tracks going up and down. Cleaning up and then taking stock.

The upstairs was completely cleaned out except for the odd bits of furniture in Horace's old rooms. The dining room and drawing room were emptied, but the kitchen was untouched—table, chairs, range, pots and pans, the everyday dishes that had once been used by the servants. And the library was ours—books, clocks, and furniture.

"It's still home," Grandmother said stoutly. "We will make do till the business turns around. It does pick up every spring."

"We always make do, Hortensia," Rose said, looking lovingly around at her kitchen with everything in its place.

Once again, we heard the grinding sound of the front bell. I rose without a word and went out.

It was Ivy. "Cook said to bring you some supper and to say she was sorry for your troubles." She handed me a small roasting pan wrapped in a quilted server to keep it warm.

"Please thank her for us, and thank you, too," I said. She nodded without looking at me, and I felt the heavy dull throb inside of too much loss.

I went back to the kitchen with our supper. There were only a few mutters of disapproval from Rose — too much sage, stuffing too dry, gravy too thick. She smacked her lips with pleasure over the shortcomings of the cook next door.

"Salty," Grandmother said. "But you see, they'll rally round us now. There's no pleasure in seeing one of your own fall. It will never do."

I bowed my head. She still believed that everything could stay the same. And it made the work I had to do all the more difficult.

Chapter Twenty-four

For the time being, making do would not be so very different from the way things had been. Grandmother took the bed in the small room that Horace had used on the coldest winter nights, next to Rose's larger room, just off the kitchen. I made up a bed on the chaise in the library. It was a comforting place to be, with so much of the house empty and echoing. But I knew the unhappy truth that Grandmother refused to see.

Grandmother did know that she couldn't take care of me or see to my schooling. But what she hadn't figured out was that she couldn't take care of herself. The shabby truth was written on every empty wall in every empty room. I had hidden the truth once, and hard as it was, I had to speak the truth now. I had to say it. Soon.

But first I was going to see Ivy Victoria. That would be tricky. If Mrs. Vandermeer saw me, I might be turned away even if I went to the back door the way Ivy had said.

But I did have the Vandermeers' supper dish to return. I'd go early, just before full light. I was pretty sure Ivy's mother was the only one who was not an early riser. It was my best chance.

I slipped out when the sky was just beginning to brighten on the edges, and hurried down the drive to the back of the house. One of the maids must have seen me pass by the kitchen window, because she was in the doorway, motioning to me. "Come in," she said in a loud whisper. "The young miss will be right down. She's always up early, takes hot chocolate with us before formal breakfast is served in the dining room." She took the dish from my hands and led me to the kitchen.

I followed her in, numbed by the sight of the servants' table and so many at the table eating before the day's work began. They all looked at me, curious-like.

"Hello," I said, not sure how to begin. "Thank you all for the grand supper."

"We're sorry for your troubles, miss," one woman

155

said. I saw the expectant looks, hopes that I would share a tidbit of something.

I nodded, but what morsel could I offer them? Our troubles were all pretty public now. I sighed with relief when Ivy popped around the corner. She stared in surprise.

"Ivy . . ." I began, and halted. I wasn't even sure she still wanted to be friends. The room went dead still. How to get it out in front of all these people, say what I needed to say? But wouldn't it be rude to get all private and brush them off? How could I do that? They were curious, but kind, too.

"Hattie, what is it?" Ivy asked in the voice of a friend who expects to hear the worst.

I swallowed. "I need your help," I admitted. "And your father's help, too."

Ivy listened thoughtfully and nodded as I poured out my heart, then squeezed one of my hands.

"Thank you," I said. Gently, I squeezed her hand back to let her know that I was her friend, too.

The next morning, I went back to Ivy's house, but I didn't go around to the back. Instead, I walked bravely to the front of the house the way Ivy had told me to do. When I reached the porch, the butler, wearing his stern face, flung open the door, but I caught the wink of encouragement.

"Did I hear the door? Who's calling at this ungodly hour?" came the shrill voice of Mrs. Vandermeer. She stood in the doorway of the dining room. Her hair was rumpled, and she was still in her dressing gown. "You?" she said haughtily, giving me a cold glare. "What are you doing here? You're not invited. Not here. Not ever. You insolent child."

I glanced around, but Ivy was nowhere in sight. Her mother had probably banished her. My heart sank, and my hope went with it. I backed toward the door. I shouldn't have come. It was all a mistake.

"Mother, stop it, please," Ivy said, seeming to come out of nowhere. "I asked Hattie here, because she's my friend. If you're going to yell, yell at me."

Mrs. Vandermeer whirled around to confront Ivy. "Go to your room. I will deal with you later. But you," she said, turning to me again, "get out of my house."

There really was nothing to do but leave. I didn't want to make more trouble for Ivy, who had shown that she was my true friend and had all the courage of a Hill

Hawk. But Ivy didn't go to her room. She came over and stood beside me and took my hand.

"Hattie is my guest, too," Mr. Vandermeer said quietly, suddenly looming up behind his wife. "Ivy, please show our friend into my study. I will be right with you."

And all my fear flew away. I knew that Ivy had spoken to him for me, the way I'd asked. He might not be able to help me, but he would be kind. He was.

Soon enough, Mr. Vandermeer sat at his desk, Ivy and I in soft leather chairs that we'd pulled close together. "Please, Hattie," he said, "feel free to speak your mind."

"Thank you, sir," I said. "It's about Grandmother."

He nodded.

"And about her house." I stopped, searching for the right words.

He nodded again in an encouraging way.

I took a deep breath. "She can't keep it now, can she? I mean, I don't see any way that she can. It's empty nearly, and she has no . . ." I stopped again, unable to say that she was nearly destitute.

"I understand," he said gently. "What is your wish, Hattie?"

I took another deep, shuddery breath. "I hoped, sir,

that you could put us in touch with a buyer. Someone honest-like, you know."

"Yes, I see your dilemma. . . ." He rolled a pen between a finger and thumb. "It will not be so difficult as you think. Indeed, I have a colleague who has expressed the desire on many occasions to purchase a property here. He will gladly pay a good price for the privilege."

I took another deep breath. "It's a lot to ask, but could you find a good place . . . a quiet street for Grandmother, and maybe, a . . . a garden spot for flowers?"

Mr. Vandermeer looked pleasantly surprised. "That will not pose a problem," he said. "There are quite a few homes on the market in very good locations."

"Thank you for your trouble, sir," I said.

"No trouble." He smiled. "It's simply the right thing to do."

I nodded, repeating his words to myself, feeling the pain of them. If only I had done the right things from the very beginning.

At teatime in the library that afternoon, I gently approached Grandmother. I had to tell her about my talk with Mr. Vandermeer and about selling the house. But how should I say it? Grandmother was still quite shaken from the tragic events of the past few days, and now I had to give her more hard news.

I sat down in my usual place next to her on the chaise while Rose poured the tea. I opened my mouth, but my voice seemed to have disappeared. I closed my mouth, swallowed hard, and searched for the kindest words.

Grandmother reached over and patted my hand. "Such a comfort to be having tea in the library together as always."

"But don't you see?" I began slowly. "It's fine for now and pleasant here in the library . . . for now," I said again.

"Whatever do you mean? What are you suggesting?" Grandmother said, her eyebrows furrowed.

I bent my head and pressed my lips together. No. No more delays. No more putting off bad news for a better time. I took a deep breath and looked up. "Grandmother," I said gently, moving to sit even closer to her, "how will you pay the taxes next year? How will you pay for gas and coal now? How will you buy food?"

"I have already said, and Cousin Ernest has said, that business will pick up in the spring." But I heard the chink of doubt creep into her voice. "What else can I do? It's the way we've always managed."

I touched her as gently as a piece of fine crystal. "Grandmother, the house is empty. All that's left are the ghosts of once-upon-a-time." I stopped, wet my lips, and went on: "But I should have asked your permission first, Grandmother."

"Permission? For what?" she said.

"I was afraid you'd say that it was out of the question, and then I couldn't have done it, but don't you see? There really is no other way." And then I blurted out the rest like my old usual self and told them how kind Mr. Vandermeer had been and how he would help find a good house in a fine neighborhood and a buyer for Grandmother's house.

For a moment there was stunned silence. Both Grandmother and Rose looked aghast. Grandmother leaned back against the chaise, her face as pale as when the sheriff had handed her the warrant.

Rose was the first to recover. "Hattie's right, Hortensia," she said. "About everything. How will the taxes get paid? We can't manage them and all the rest any more than we could run a boarding house."

"I cannot leave my house," Grandmother said. "These

walls, this room, my flower garden in summer. My Lily was born in this house. I will not let anyone take it away." And then she did something I had never seen her do: she cried.

"No one can take our dearest treasures, Grandmother," I said softly. Then I got up and went to the bookshelf and took *Alice* from her place. "You should have this, Grandmother." And I gave her the letter that Grandfather had written to my mother.

Grandmother unfolded the letter, her eyes skimming over the lines. "'. . . the dearest treasure,'" she whispered.

"Treasure no one can take away," I said. "Not as long as our hearts keep beating. Maybe never." I knew this to be a true fact. My heart was filled every day with Ma and Pa, my friend Jasper back home, and all my good times here with Grandmother and Rose and Horace. And now Ivy, too. But hanging on to bad times and hurtful people like Aggie and Effie, who wouldn't or couldn't forgive? No. They were for letting go. No place in my heart for those.

Rose got up and sat on the other side of Grandmother. "It's time, Hortensia," she said. "Hattie is right. It's time."

Chapter Twenty-five

As it turned out, Mr. Vandermeer did have a good buyer for the house. And more. He helped us to find a suitable house filled with light in a good neighborhood not so very far down the hill from Grandmother's old society world. The houses here were smaller and closer together, but there was a yard for a garden—flowers for Grandmother, vegetables for Rose—the sort of place where they could be happy. And the cherished things that Grandmother had had left after the auction were just enough to fill the rooms.

Surprisingly, Rose clucked like a mother hen over the nooks and crannies and gadgets in her new kitchen, which was quite up-to-date. She clattered and banged and had a jolly time settling in. I even caught her singing, not exactly on key, but happily. And Grandmother did concede that at her age, a smaller house was much easier to keep up. Indeed, there was something to be said for a cozy nest, she avowed. She seemed content, grudgingly happy, as she planned the layout of her garden.

Once we were settled in and Horace came by to visit with baskets of teas and meats and tins of food, and Ivy stopped by with her father (which opened the way for others from the old days to call on Grandmother, too), things looked brighter again for all of us.

As spring came on and the flowers bloomed and filled the house with their bright colors and fragrances, the gray disappeared entirely from the old ones' faces. Grandmother was restored, not quite to her former glory, but glory enough, she said, as one by one, friends from the old days, and even a few who were new, began to call. Then I knew it was time.

I took up my tablet and began to write:

Dear Pa,

You're probably out on the river again rafting logs, making those river trips and having a grand old time. A lot has changed here these past few months, and I have a lot of things to confess about my misdeeds and our misfortunes. But mainly now, Pa, I need you to come, please, and take me home.

I want you to know that I passed the Regents exams, but there's no money now for tuition. What I want is to earn money to pay my own way and go to the Academy in the fall. I want to learn, Pa. I know it is the right thing for me, but I need a good dose of home, too.

I would be especially grateful if you could ask around if anyone would need a good worker for the summer for housekeeping and such in Pepacton or Downsville. Well, I am still no cook, and I am young, but you know, Pa, that I am not afraid to work. I know things have changed at home, too, but I will help your new wife however I can, and you too, Pa. I know you're farming some, and I can help with the barn chores and the garden and putting up preserves.

I hate to be asking so much, but when you come, please bring overalls and a good sturdy shirt. I reckon I'll be needing them for the walk back over the mountains to home.

Your loving daughter,

Hattie Belle Basket

ACKNOWLEDGMENTS

Thanks and love to my husband, Stephen Jennings, for everything—listening, caring, kindness—and for the extra help with researching laws and legal procedures of the 19th century. YOTLA

Andrea Tompa—editor and treasured friend—thank you for walking with me through the forest, lighting the dark path.

Librarian Audra Everett for research assistance and the librarians in the Western Sullivan Public Library system for the ongoing support—thank you.